BETTY

GEORGES SIMENON

Translated by Alastair Hamilton

A Helen and Kurt Wolff Book

B

ETTY

Harcourt Brace Jovanovich New York and London

7/2/81

Printed in the United States of America

Library of Congress Cataloging in Publication Data

Simenon, Georges, 1903–
    Betty.

    "A Helen and Kurt Wolff book."
    I. Title.
PZ3.S5892Bh3   [PQ2637.I53]   843'.9'12   74–22072
ISBN 0–15–111923–6

First edition

B C D E

Illustrations by Marie Hickman

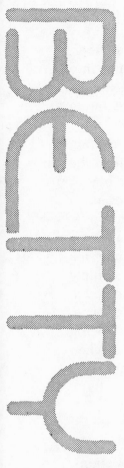BETTY

"Would you like something to eat?"

She shook her head. She had the impression that there was something unnatural about the voice she heard. It was as though it came from behind a windowpane.

"Of course, when I say 'something to eat' that means rabbit. As you can see, today is rabbit day. It's too bad

71286

if you don't like it. When it's a cod day there's nothing but cod. . . ."

It was curious to hear one syllable after another, each syllable fastening on to the next, turning into words, into sentences, rather like thread which gradually turns into lace or wool which turns into a knitted stocking.

The image of an unfinished knitted stocking, hanging from its three needles, made her smile. She didn't expect to imagine such a commonplace object, here, in front of a man who was obviously eager to appear distinguished and who took such care over constructing his sentences. He was dressed in gray. Everything about him was gray: his eyes, his hair, his skin, even his tie and his shirt. There wasn't a single spot of color. And, as she listened to him, she started to think not about a gray stocking but about a black one, because all the stockings she had ever seen being knitted were black, a long time ago, in Vendée, when she was still under fourteen. And now she was twenty-eight. . . .

"It's a question of habit."

She almost asked:

"What's a question of habit?"

For her mind was wandering in several directions. She couldn't see the connection between habit and the woolen stocking, and she had forgotten that the stocking was in her own mind and not in that of the man sitting opposite her. Yet her face must have betrayed the question for the man continued with insistent determination:

"Liking or disliking."

Liking what? She had forgotten the rabbit and the cod. Once again her eyes met those of an American officer sitting on one of the stools at the bar. He had been looking at her the whole time and she wondered where she had seen him before.

"Wednesday is stew day, or maybe I should say stew evening."

She gathered from the man's thin smile that he had made a subtle distinction, and she would have liked to have followed him.

"Do you like it?"

Like it? She could no longer understand a word of this conversation and it was becoming increasingly comic. Everything was getting mixed up with everything else. But that was too bad. She said solemnly: "Yes."

She had no idea what he was talking about but she didn't want to be rude. She didn't know this excessively well-dressed man with a fascinatingly sharp expression. She didn't even know his name. Yet she was closer to him than she had ever been to anyone, really, for apart from him there was absolutely nothing left.

It sounded odd, but that was how it was. It could go on for any amount of time, for an hour, a night, or longer. And this made her smile a smile which, for the moment at least, lacked bitterness. He was very polite. He hadn't made a pass at her in the car and he hadn't asked her a single personal question.

For she remembered the car, the soft, cool leather

upholstery, the rain on the windshield and the misted windows on which she had automatically done a drawing with her finger tips. She recalled the lights of the town which had been concentrated in every drop of water, and then the headlights on the expressway. She could have given a detailed account of everything that had happened since, the sort of account required by an examining magistrate or a doctor.

Of everything that had happened since when? Since the bar on Rue de Ponthieu, anyhow. It would be too unpleasant to go any farther back and she refused to do so. She didn't want to spoil something which had been so hard to obtain and which was going to be still harder to preserve: this state of perfect balance, or rather of perfect suspension, a pleasant, restful, almost lighthearted state of suspension.

Of course, it wasn't lighthearted in the normal sense of the word. She didn't want to break out laughing or to start dancing or telling stories. The marvelous thing about it was that she had absolutely no idea of what would happen next, that same evening, or the next day, or any other day, and she couldn't care less.

"It always amazes me that people who eat animals every day never stop to think. . . ."

She was listening, staring into the eyes of the man whom she saw as though he were behind a magnifying glass. But, for all her good intentions, other thoughts continued to trickle into her mind.

Before leaving Rue de Ponthieu she should have asked him to wait while she went to the lavatory, where the attendant would certainly have had a pair of stockings to sell her. They almost all have.

It bothered her to have a run on each leg. For the first time in her life, she hadn't changed her stockings for ages. Two days? Three days? She didn't want to know how many. She hadn't had a bath either, and that, too, would soon be a source of embarrassment. Would there be a bathtub and would he give her time to use it?

She saw faces, some close, some farther away, hair, eyes, noses, mouths moving, and she heard voices which weren't necessarily connected with those mouths. She tried to make out what sort of a place they had come to, but she couldn't manage it and instinctively raised her glass of whisky.

"Cheers."

There was a blond waitress behind the bar with large breasts, the sort of breasts she had wanted to have when she was a little girl. There was also a smiling Negro with a white hat who appeared first in one doorway and then in another, and whom everybody appeared to know. Then there was the American officer leaning against the bar, a glass permanently clasped in his hands, who continued to gaze at her.

Some people were eating and others were just drinking, in groups or on their own, staring into space in silence.

"Had it never occurred to you that we were actually full of animals?"

She knew she was drunk. She had been drunk for

some time, but at the moment she was getting really high: she didn't feel ill, she didn't want to be sick, and she didn't want to cry. Was the man drunk too? Had he been drinking before they met at the Ponthieu?

He had arrived suddenly, out of the dark street, with drops of rain on his tweed suit. He was obviously a regular patron there, too, one could sense that from the way he looked round the room and greeted the barman.

She had been sitting on a stool and he had asked if he could sit next to her.

"By all means."

His hands were very thin, long and pale, and he played with them the whole time as though they were objects separate from himself.

He didn't know where she had come from or how much she had been drinking, either. Maybe he hadn't noticed the runs in her stockings. At all events, he couldn't guess that she hadn't had a bath and that she hadn't even been able to wash after the man of that afternoon.

They were no longer on Rue de Ponthieu. She didn't know where they were. She had only been able to recognize Avenue de Versailles where she had caught a glimpse of her mother's house, then they had taken the expressway and had turned off to the right onto a dirt road. When she got out of the car, she had smelled the damp leaves and had jumped over a puddle. There was still some water in her left shoe.

They must have been in a restaurant for people were eating. There was a bar, too. There was also the sound of muffled music from a phonograph to which nobody was listening. Yet she still felt that this wasn't a normal kind of establishment and that everybody was looking at her.

All those people, including the American officer, seemed to know each other, even though they didn't talk to each other, and the owner went from table to table, sitting down from time to time, without taking his eyes off her. Her hair wasn't untidy. She didn't have smut on her nose. Her suit was perfectly all right. Admittedly, there were her stockings, but runs happen to all women.

Maybe she had to be introduced and accepted. Or perhaps she had to pass some sort of test.

"Is everything all right, doctor?"

This time the owner was talking to the man she was with, but he didn't sit down and the man simply blinked without bothering to reply, looked again at his hands lying flat on the table, and started to scratch meticulously at the skin between his fingers.

"You're not listening. . . ."

He was talking to her, for the owner had already moved somewhere else.

"Yes, I am."

"What was I saying?"

"That by eating so many animals . . ."

He gazed at her and she wondered whether that was the correct answer. She must have annoyed him because he got up, muttering:

"Excuse me for a second."

He strode toward one of the doors. The owner came up and collected the two empty glasses.

"The same again?"

She felt she had seen him before, too. It had become a mania that evening. Not only as far as people were concerned, but also objects. It all reminded her of something. But when? And where?

"Is this the first time you've been to The Hole?"

"Yes."

She didn't know that the place was called "The Hole" and she wondered whether it was a joke or a trap, and whether she should have taken the question seriously.

"Have you known the doctor long?"

"No."

"Don't you want anything to eat?"

"No, thank you. I'm not hungry."

"Do as you like. Everyone does as he likes here."

She smiled at him in order to thank him for talking to her and, to proclaim her composure, drank half the contents of her glass, opened her handbag, and powdered her face. Her face was swollen. She did not like to look in the little mirror in which she could also see a very dark, very large woman sitting behind her.

"When you know the place better, you won't be able to stop coming."

Her companion, a curiously concentrated expression on his face, had sat down opposite her again.

"I'm sorry I left you on your own."

She tried vainly to hear what the people behind her were saying, convinced that they were talking about her. Then she, too, got up and murmured:

"Do you mind?"

On her way to the lavatory, she suddenly found herself standing opposite the Negro who looked at her, laughing silently, as if meeting her in a narrow corridor were incredibly funny. But he did nothing to her, stepped aside, laughing still more, and she came out into a dirty and untidy kitchen. A door which didn't shut properly led to the lavatory with its window giving onto the open countryside.

She started to feel impatient, for no special reason. Perhaps she felt a little frightened, too. It was time she had another drink, to stay on the surface before being engulfed by anxiety or sadness.

When she came back to the cocktail lounge, she swallowed what remained of her whisky before she even sat down.

"I'm thirsty," she sighed.

Her companion called:

"Joseph! Give the lady a drink."

"The same again?"

She said yes.

"For you, too, doctor?"

"May as well."

Again she wanted to get it over with, she wanted to lie down, either on her own or with someone else, anywhere, and close her eyes. The music, the din, tired her. She was fed up with seeing faces, eyes looking at her as though she were a freak or an intruder.

"Why are you scratching yourself?"

She was obviously a little slow on the uptake.

"Me?" she asked in amazement, after what seemed to her a very long time.

Perhaps she had scratched the back of her hand. She hadn't noticed it. But the man grabbed her wrist with a contained avidity, an expression of unexpectedly childish joy on his face.

"It's here, isn't it?"

He indicated an invisible point.

"Yes . . . I suppose so. . . ."

"Under the skin?"

He alarmed her and she continued to say yes in order not to annoy him.

"Is it climbing?"

"Is what climbing?"

"Is it revolving on the surface or inside the flesh? This is very important because they all have different characteristics. I know of some that . . ."

"What are you talking about?"

"The worms."

"What worms?"

"Ah, do you still not realize that you have worms under your skin? Worms of every sort; tiny ones and large ones, fat ones and thin ones, restless ones and placid ones? You undoubtedly also have other little animals, infinitely more subtle ones, which I will show you and whose nature I will reveal to you. . . ."

She could now see the thin, colorless face close to her own, the sleek gray hair, the eyes of an almost identical gray, and she was suddenly aware of the fact that something abnormal was happening. She wanted to withdraw her hand. She tried, but he held it firmly.

"You'll see how I trace down those little animals that torture us so diabolically. . . ."

With his free hand, he produced from his pocket a gold toothpick with a sharp point.

"Don't be frightened. I know what I'm doing."

A voice said:

"Leave her alone, doctor."

"I'm just removing a little worm that is making her suffer and . . ."

The owner came a step closer and laid his hand in a friendly manner on the doctor's shoulder.

"Come with me a moment."

"Wait a minute. She asked me . . ."

"Come along. . . ."

"Why?"

"Something confidential."

The gray man looked up hesitantly.

"Are you afraid I'm going to hurt her? You're forgetting that . . ."

His smile was bitter, resigned. Yet he was a big man, while the owner was small and thickset. A second later he was on his feet, his toothpick in his hand, humiliated, and he let himself be pushed toward the back door.

Betty looked at her hands nervously. She drained her glass and then, with a shrug of her shoulders, that of her companion. She still didn't know who he was. She knew nothing. She knew nothing any more and she started to feel panic. The American officer at the bar looked at her lugubriously, without smiling.

"Waiter!"

"Yes, madam."

"Give me a drink."

He no longer asked her if she wanted the same thing. She was in a hurry. The sooner she got it over with the better. The images were getting blurred. There was a head of red hair, for example, which could have been close to her or at the other end of the room, and she didn't know whether it was a man's or a woman's. She had to make an effort to focus her eyes, and when she did she saw fixed, indifferent faces which might have been made of wax.

They must have disapproved of her though she couldn't understand why.

She must have made a mistake, broken the rules of the house. How could she have done otherwise since she didn't know the rules? Why wasn't she told what they were?

It wasn't by drinking that she gave offense. The proof was that the manager himself had summoned the waiter the first time and that the others were drinking as much as, if not more than, she was. A young woman with mouse-colored hair sitting on the edge of a bench had turned deathly pale and her companion, who was holding her hand affectionately, appeared not to notice anything.

What would happen if Betty were to start shouting? She was tempted to do so in order to see what would happen, in order to change things, in order to get people to take some trouble over her instead of just looking at her.

What if she were to tell them all she had done over the last three days? Would those faces at last take on a human expression? Would there be compassion or simply a slight interest in all those fishlike eyes?

Her hand trembled as she groped in her bag.

"Waiter!"

"Yes, madam. The same again?"

That proved once more that it wasn't because of what she was drinking.

"Have you got any cigarettes?"

"Just a minute."

A motor could be heard outside. The sound of a car, which had had some difficulty in getting out of the mud, faded away in the distance. A voice said:

"Mario will drive him home."

At first Betty didn't realize that those words were addressed to her, for they came from behind her back. At almost the same time, she saw a woman's hand offering her a cigarette.

She turned around. The large dark-haired woman, who had a white streak in her hair, was standing next to her, and, touching the chair where the doctor had been sitting, was saying:

"May I?"

She had a hoarse voice and gray pearls around her neck. Betty must have had one whisky too many because the images were becoming increasingly blurred, as they had that afternoon in the bedroom, before the man got dressed again. She hadn't seen him leave. He could have taken her handbag, her clothes. He could have strangled her, and she wouldn't have been able to give a description of him. Of course, she couldn't if he had strangled her. But . . .

She was getting muddled. The sounds were all

merging together. Her body, on the chair, had started swaying and she could no longer control it. If it swayed any more she would fall onto the floor, amid the feet and the cigarette ends. She really would be dirty then!

"Did he upset you?" Who? Why? She had almost forgotten the man in gray.

"He's a charming fellow as well as being a man of real merit."

The woman had brought her glass with her.

"Cheers."

"Cheers."

"I hope you realize that he takes drugs. When he left you a few minutes ago, he gave himself a shot, and it wasn't the first one this evening. Do you know him?"

"No."

"He's called Bernard. He was a doctor in Versailles."

A doctor in Versailles. She still heard the words and grasped their meaning. What escaped her was the connection the words could have with her. Why did the other woman tell her all this so solemnly, as though it were important or dramatic? And she, at least, must have noticed the runs on her stockings. Perhaps she had perceived that she wasn't very clean under her make-up.

She had beautiful dark eyes, and her deep, broken voice was reassuring.

Betty tried to close her eyes in order to concentrate, but she had to open them again immediately because everything started spinning.

"I'm thirsty," she murmured.

She was handed a glass, her own or someone else's, it didn't make much difference.

"Have you had dinner?"

"I think so."

"Aren't you hungry?"

"No."

"Don't you want a breath of air?"

"No."

She couldn't go outside because she was incapable of walking. If she tried to stand up, she was sure to fall down. She would fall down anyhow, of course, sooner or later, but she didn't want it to happen while she was still conscious.

What did it matter where she woke up, in hospital or anywhere else! It might even be better if she never woke up at all. She really believed that. She wasn't sad. She had been beyond sadness for a long time.

"You've made a hit with Alan. He hasn't taken his eyes off you since you came in, and he doesn't realize that he's drinking his eighth whisky."

Betty forced herself to smile, like somebody well-mannered who is listening.

"I can hear Mario coming back."

She could hear a car too, then a door slamming, and the noise of the rain past the open door of the restaurant. Which car was it? . . . That was a problem. If Mario had taken the doctor's car . . .

"Did you manage to put him to bed?"

"His wife helped me."

"He didn't make too much of a fuss, did he?"

"He's already counting the rabbits running into his room."

She saw a look of complicity in their eyes and she knew they were referring to her: the dark woman shrugged her shoulders slightly as if to say that it wasn't serious. She didn't mind and she didn't try to work out what they were planning.

She repeated pointlessly:

"Rabbits . . ."

And, thinking it was a question, the dark woman explained:

"When he's like that he sees every kind of animal all over the place, not to mention the little worms crawling under his skin that he tries to extract with his toothpick. When he was still practicing, toward the end, he told his patients that all their ills were caused by those invisible worms, and he tried to dispose of them. . . ."

Who? What? Dispose of what? It was too late now. One glass ago, perhaps even one sip ago, she could have remained in that state of euphoria she had been in the whole evening.

But now her body was aching. Everywhere and nowhere! She was dirty. She was wretched. She had nobody, nobody in the world. She had signed. She had given them away. Not even given them: sold them, since she had accepted the check. A correct, official statement. The notary had dictated the terms over the telephone.

The undersigned, Elisabeth Etamble . . .

She had had to start again on a fresh sheet of paper because she had written "Betty" the first time.

The undersigned, Elisabeth Etamble, born Fayet, twenty-eight years of age, no profession, domiciled at 22 bis Avenue de Wagram in Paris, admits . . .

How could she not have admitted it, since it was true and she had been caught red-handed?

Her glass was empty again. It was always empty. She looked for the waiter, slightly ashamed of ordering a drink in front of this woman whom she didn't know.

"I need to get plastered," she explained.

Then she added, because of the vulgarity of the word she had used:

"I'm sorry."

"I know how it is."

She didn't know anything. But it didn't matter.

"The same again, waiter."

And she suddenly started to explain volubly, tripping over syllables just as one trips over steps:

"You see, I didn't know him at all. We were introduced to each other a little while ago by some friends in a bar . . ."

She hadn't been introduced to him any more than she had been introduced to the man that afternoon or to the one the day before. Why did she feel the need to make things up?

Because she was talking to a woman?

Besides, the woman obviously didn't believe her. She nodded in approval, but she did so out of politeness, because she was well brought up.

The pale girl had gone to sleep on the edge of the bench, and the man she was with had disengaged his hand and was smoking a cigarette and talking to the owner.

It wouldn't be so easy for Betty. To start with, there was nobody to hold her hand. Then, she was going to be ill. It was only a matter of minutes, she was well aware of that. She was swaying more and more, so much so that she held on to the table, although she didn't appear to be doing so.

"Do you live near here?"

She shook her head, but took care not to shake it too much.

"In Paris?"

Not in Paris or anywhere else. She didn't live anywhere. What was this woman going on about? If she hadn't sat down at her table, it would probably have been the American. He must have had a car parked outside. He would have taken Betty somewhere where there was a bed. He, too, might have asked her some questions, but she could have told him anything she liked and he would have been moved.

She might not even have been ill if she had gone with him, if only out of pride and because of the fact that she would at last have had a bath.

She didn't know what the time was. She hadn't known what the time was for three days and three nights, and daylight and darkness had lost all meaning for her. Everything was in a muddle.

The dark woman opposite her was talking in a

whisper and she sounded as though she were praying in church.

"The bald man smoking a cigar on your left is an English lord with an estate at Louveciennes and every night . . ."

The woman must have been twenty years older than she was. She seemed to have had a great deal of experience, to have known all sorts of people, especially peculiar people.

She suddenly heard a shout.

She hadn't been thinking. She should have asked her to help her, she should have said something like:

"Hold on to me, please . . . do something, anything. . . ."

It must stop! She must stop thinking! Somebody must hold her hand, put her to bed, watch over her while she slept. Somebody, a human being, must be there when she opened her eyes.

Had she really said something? Had her throat emitted a sound? She was almost sure she had said:

"Madame!"

Nobody was asking her questions any more. Nobody was asking her anything. There was no surprise, no curiosity on the face opposite her. Yet she wasn't in a hospital or in an asylum where one is used to patients sitting up in bed to call for help, was she?

She was in a restaurant. Men and women were drinking. However blurred her vision, they were there and the sound of glasses, the phonograph, the voices were real.

But it seemed to her that she had lost contact with the others, that they couldn't hear her, or that, for some mysterious reason, they didn't want to hear her.

She was in their midst, but she didn't exist any more than she had existed that afternoon in the street. People had gone by, one after the other. Some had brushed against her or even bumped into her, but not one of them had noticed that she was a living being.

"You understand?"

She had written out the statement, all the words that had been dictated to her. She had signed it. She had made the effort to put "Elisabeth" instead of "Betty." She had stuffed the check into her bag and it must still be there. She had . . .

It was too much. She couldn't stand it any longer. She groped for the glass on the table. But she dropped it, clumsily, and it broke on the red tiles on the floor.

She started to say:

"I'm . . ."

She wanted to say:

"I'm sorry."

Instead of that, she clenched her fists and yelled:

"No! No! No! No!"

It was all over. Over! There was a limit to everything. She was aware that everybody was looking at her, but she couldn't see anyone in particular, nothing but a mass of expressionless flesh.

"You couldn't care less, could you?"

She tried to laugh, and at the same time she was sobbing. She tried to get up but she fell onto the floor, although she didn't break like the glass. There was a table leg two inches away from her nose, and she was surrounded by chair legs and by the feet of men and women.

She was ashamed of behaving so badly and if she had been strong enough, she would have apologized. She knew she shouldn't have shouted, that she was drunk, that she shouldn't have had that last glass.

The table, the chairs moved away from her. She was being held by her shoulders. Her feet dragged along the ground and she recognized the piles of dirty plates in the kitchen. She was sure the Negro was there. She tried to see him, but she couldn't.

She heard people talking but she made no effort to understand what they were saying. She groaned gently because she really was in pain.

"Have you got a bandage?"

"There must be one in the drawer."

"What shall we do with her?"

"What do you think?"

"I'll take her."

"You?"

"Why not?"

"To the Carlton?"

She felt a still sharper pain in her hand when they disinfected the cut made by a piece of glass.

"Don't you think she needs a doctor?"

"Why should she?"

"Are you in a fit state to drive?"

"Just put her in my car."

She thought she was unconscious. She didn't know that she was taking everything in, that she would find all these words, with the same intonation, in her memory, the noises in the cocktail lounge, in the kitchen, even the smell of rabbit mingled with the smell of liquor and cigarettes.

She would recall the taste of the rain on her lips, other smells, too, the smell of the car, of her wet hair, a smell of cows somewhere.

"Be careful when you go into reverse."

"Yes."

"You've got a good two yards . . . Go ahead . . . Stop!"

The car leapt forward and the dark woman lit a cigarette with one hand.

Rain. Trees. Lights. Cobbles.

Then a doorway with tall white columns and two men in blue uniforms who hurried forward.

"Put my friend in room 53. She isn't feeling well."

Her head wobbled helplessly as she was carried in, and the elevator rose gently.

BETTY

2

Her eyelashes fluttered but her lids didn't open wide enough to let the images in. At the same time, the sulky expression left her lips and, with a vague, lazy gesture, she raised her hand and pushed back the hair which was covering almost her entire face and tickling her cheek.

Refusing to open her eyes, she curled up, searching for the comfort of her own heat, her smell, the movement of her blood in her veins, the rhythmic passage of air into her nostrils which contracted with each breath.

She had instinctively assumed the position of a child in its mother's womb, as if to protect herself, to form a complete, united, impregnable whole.

She already knew a great many things which she didn't want to know yet and she deliberately pushed them aside, into an indefinite area she used to call limbo.

As a child, it had been an agreeable, sometimes even a sensual game that she liked to play, especially when she was in bed with flu and had a high enough temperature to obtain the required effect.

Today it seemed to her that to remain in this state of pseudo-innocence was a vital necessity.

She had a headache, not a particularly violent one, not nearly as violent as she had expected: a dull pain of which she could vary the intensity and the nature by pressing her head at various angles into the pillow.

She was thirsty, but in order to drink she would have had to emerge from her state of torpor, open her eyes, face up to reality.

She preferred to keep her thirst. It was accompanied by a taste that reminded her of the first time she had had a child, when she had been so frightened that she had been given an injection to make her numb. Now, too, all her mucous membranes were more sensitive, more tender than usual, and she had the recurrent impression that they were swelling, that her whole body was swelling, was becoming so light that she could float in space.

She had been given an injection that night, she could remember it perfectly well.

"You can leave us, Lucien."

"Are you sure you don't need anything? Don't you want me to call the maid?"

The room she was in had not been aired for several days and it had a musty smell about it. Not the stale smell you get in town, but the smell you get in the country that reminds you of wet hay. When the porter and the doorman had wanted to turn on the light, the dark-haired woman had said to them:

"No! She mustn't have too much light. Leave me alone with her. Just open the door of my room."

The sound of the men's steps had faded away. Betty was lying on top of the bedspread. The woman had gone into the adjoining room where, judging from the sound, she must have taken off her clothes. Did she think that Betty was going to be sick all over her dress or tear it by clinging to her?

Betty had been tempted to cheat, to open her eyes for a second. She hadn't done it and she may well have been incapable of doing it. The dark woman came back, undressed her expertly, taking everything off, her slip, her brassiere, her stockings, then, after a moment's hesitation, her tight transparent nylon pants.

She went into the bathroom, ran the water, and, with

the skill of a nurse, passed the sponge covered with soap over Betty's face and body and rinsed her with lukewarm water mixed with eau de Cologne.

She said nothing, she didn't mutter to herself, but she occasionally, inadvertently, hummed some snatches from a tune that had been played on the phonograph during most of the evening.

"There you are," she sighed at last. "Now try and get some rest and stop worrying.

She managed to pull down the bed covers without moving Betty off and gently shifted her body onto fresh, lightly starched sheets.

Did she know that Betty was taking everything in and that she would remember everything? What sort of expression did she have on her face as she gazed at her by the light of a single lamp at the other end of the room?

Betty hadn't dreamed it all. Nor had she dreamed the words that came back to her memory, their exact intonation, the sounds and the smells which went with them.

"What do you think?"

"I'll take her."

"You?"

"Why not?"

It was Mario, the owner of The Hole, who had been talking to the dark woman, and their intimacy, their familiarity, the way they understood each other's allusions had struck Betty.

"Are you in a fit state to drive?"

Mario had something plebeian about him. He was stocky and slightly insolent. He gave the impression of calm strength, and when he sat down with his patrons, he seemed to be taking them under his wing. Had he not appeared at the very moment when the doctor, obsessed by his little animals, had started to be obnoxious and perhaps even dangerous?

He hadn't been angry, he hadn't even raised his voice. Firmly, but without any brutality, he had freed the young woman and had driven the doctor home.

"Did you manage to put him to bed?"

"His wife helped me."

There was no irony in his voice, barely a note of amusement when he said:

"He's already counting the rabbits running into his room."

Betty was looking more dead than alive. She thought she had reached the depths of despair and yet, at that moment, she had wondered whether Mario was the lover of the dark woman or simply a friend.

She recalled other images, more clearly and in greater detail than when she had actually seen them, the blonde barmaid, for instance, with her provocative breasts: she had a huge mole on her cheek and she constantly passed her hands over her hips as though her garter belt were slipping up. She must have had milky skin that bruised easily and which, when she undressed, retained the mark of the elastic and fasteners.

At one point the lamp had been switched off. All that

remained was a faint light coming from the open door of the adjoining room where the dark woman hadn't gone to bed yet, but was walking to and fro smoking a cigarette that had a very precise smell, different from what cigarettes usually smelled like. Water was running in a bathtub.

Betty was really ill. Her heart was beating fast and irregularly, and she sometimes thought that it would never resume its normal beat. What would happen then? Would she die? Just like that, from one moment to the next, without noticing it? She didn't call for help. She had made up her mind not to call, to die alone if need be, and she was pleased to know that her body was clean at last. Not completely. Almost. The damp sponge had even been passed between her toes.

How long had this been going on? She groaned, she was aware of groaning in spite of her efforts not to and she hoped that the sound was too faint to be heard.

She hoped, above all, that the lady was asleep. It was pitch dark. Betty was no longer sure of her senses. Did she really hear the sound of slippers on the floor, the sound of somebody breathing and coming nearer and nearer? Did a hot hand take hold of her wrist? Did a voice, her voice, say:

"*I'm scared.*"

"*Shh! . . . You mustn't worry. . . .*"

Somebody took her pulse. She was aware that somebody was taking her pulse, not once but twice, at least, maybe even three times, with intervals of immobility and silence as in the room of somebody very seriously ill.

There was no sound in the hotel, no sound outside other than the patter of the rain on the shutters which were occasionally shaken by a gust of wind. She didn't dare ask for light.

The light came a little later, not in her room but next door, where, for some mysterious reason, an alcohol burner was lit. She recognized the smell. Her father, a manufacturer of chemical products, used to sell liquid fuel. He had been a lively man with red hair, who used to make fun of his customers and imitate them behind their backs. He invented cleaning products. It was too bad that the Germans had shot him at the end of the war. No one ever knew why.

A hand pulled down the bedspread and Betty felt a needle going into her thigh, a liquid slowly flowing into her.

It was like the first time she had had a child. She had refused the second time. It may have been the same drug. She felt a sense of well-being almost immediately, a sense of numbness which still left some live particles in her mind.

Someone was holding her hand. Her pulse was taken once more. She must have been sweating because she heard the tap running and, a little later, a cold towel was put over her forehead and her eyes.

She would have liked to say thank you, if her lips had moved, but she wasn't sure of them and they made no sound.

After that there was nothing. Then, much later, something else happened which might have been real and which might have been unreal. It was impossible to tell because she had had a great many dreams. But why, if she had dreamed it, would she only have remembered this particular dream, and simply have retained an unpleasant impression and no image from the other ones?

It was almost morning. It must have been morning because she heard the waiter in the corridor, taking the breakfast trays to the various rooms.

She could have sworn that she smelled coffee and that when she opened her eyes—if she had opened them—she saw streaks of light behind the curtains. It must have been dawn, or already daytime.

She had tried to identify a sound in the next room, through the half-open door, a sound of hurried, excited breathing, and she had gotten up in order to see what was going on. She had taken a few steps, her head suddenly reeling, and, on the bed, she had seen two naked bodies making love.

Was it possible that they hadn't heard her, that they hadn't noticed her, that she had gone straight back to bed without making a sound, and that she had fallen asleep again almost immediately?

She couldn't answer the question. In her mind the man was Mario and he had a very hairy body. How long ago did all that take place? How late in the day was it now?

She didn't want to worry about that and she tried to recover her state of torpor and unconsciousness. Once or twice she saw her father, his white coverall soiled with colored stains, in his workshop on Avenue de

Versailles, cluttered with casks and demijohns smelling of paraffin oil and acid.

She had spent her childhood in that smell which drifted up to their apartment on the second floor and which her father carried wherever he went in the folds of his clothes and in his flaming red hair.

In her first year at school her neighbor, a girl with a lisp, had asked to change places, saying:

"She stinks too much."

Her breathing grew slower, more regular. Her lips opened over her little teeth which her mother called mouse teeth. Her hand had gradually slipped over her belly and, as she was to do when whe was a little girl, she stroked herself, without even realizing that she was doing it, perhaps in order to isolate herself still more from the outer world, so that all that existed was the universe of her warm flesh and her sensations.

She had been asleep for some time when she heard the floor boards creak and opened her eyes without stopping to think whether she ought to open them or not. She saw the dark woman standing between the door and the bed in a dressing gown, looking even larger than the day before.

Had Betty seen her standing up the day before? She had sat down at her table immediately and later Betty, her eyes closed, was unable to . . .

"Did I wake you up?"

"I don't know."

"I wondered whether you needed anything. How do you feel?"

"Very well."

It was true. Her headache had gone. She was weary, agreeably weary, with a slightly empty feeling in her stomach.

"I think I'm hungry."

"What would you like to eat?"

She wanted bacon and eggs, maybe because she had bacon and eggs for breakfast every time she went to a hotel. It would never have occurred to her to have them at home. And besides, her husband . . .

She didn't want to think about that just yet.

"Do you think I can?"

"Why not? I'll call the waiter."

"Have you had breakfast yet?"

"A long time ago."

"Is it late?"

"Four o'clock."

"In the afternoon?"

The question was absurd.

"How do you want your eggs? Well done?"

"Yes."

"Tea? Coffee?"

"Coffee."

"With cream?"

"Black."

The woman went to the door to tell the waiter.

"Would you like me to open the shutters?"

She pulled the curtains, leaned out to push back the shutters, and one could see the rain falling on the leaves of the trees.

"You gave me an injection, didn't you?"

"You noticed it? Don't worry. My husband was a doctor and I often stood in as his nurse during the twenty-eight years we spent together."

"I thought I was dying last night."

She didn't say that in order to be pitied but because she suddenly thought it. It was true. She could have died. And she wouldn't have been in existence anymore by now. They would have had to get her identity card out of her handbag in order to find her name and address. They would have telephoned Guy. Would he have organized the funeral or would he have left it to his brother? What would they have told Charlotte?

Instead of that, she was in bed in a cozy room with pale blue walls and a bust of Marie Antoinette on the white marble mantle.

"Would you like a bath before you have breakfast? If I know Jules, he'll take a good twenty minutes before it's ready. Don't get up at once. I'll run the water."

She was smoking from a long cigarette holder which Betty hadn't seen the night before. Her dressing gown and slippers were made of red velvet and she had done her hair and made up her face.

While the bathtub was filling, she disappeared for a second into her room and came back with a glass in her hand.

"Do you mind? Does it upset you if I have a drink?"

"Please go ahead."

"It's about this time that I feel I need one. I'm like

poor Bernard with his injections. There comes a time when you can't do anything else."

Betty wondered whether she was saying all this to put her at her ease, to stop her feeling ashamed of what happened the previous evening. She also wondered whether she had dreamed the scene on the bed and she was increasingly sure that she had not.

"Your bath is ready. If it embarrasses you . . ."

"No."

Wasn't it she who had undressed and washed her? Still, just when she was getting out of bed, she felt slightly ashamed because it seemed to her that her body gave off a smell of men.

The other woman stood by the window without looking at her. She didn't follow her into the bathroom and spoke from far away, like an actor speaking in the wings.

"The water isn't too hot, is it?"

"It's perfect."

"Are you feeling dizzy?"

"Just a bit."

She was in a worse state than she had thought. As long as she had been lying down she hadn't felt anything, but once she stood up she felt dizzy and had a sharp pain on one side of her head.

"Do you need anything?"

"No, thanks. I'm so ashamed of causing you all this trouble."

"Not at all. I'm so . . ."

She almost said:

"I'm so used to it . . ."

But she didn't finish the sentence. Only somewhat later did she go on:

"I've been through so much! And I saw so many things with my husband. I hope you're not going to fall asleep in the bath."

"No."

"I put a new toothbrush and some toothpaste by the washbasin. I always keep some in my room. It may be a hotel, but I treat it as my home. You see, I've been living here for three years. Don't worry about your underthings. Louisette, the maid, is washing them and she'll bring them back in a moment or two."

There was a knock on the door.

"Put the tray here, Jules. And while you're at it, bring me a large bottle of Perrier."

Betty wrapped herself in the terry-cloth bathrobe, ran her fingers through her hair, and walked barefoot into the room.

"Let me bring you a pair of slippers."

Her head was spinning and, now that the eggs and bacon were in front of her, she wondered whether she would be able to eat them.

"Here. Put your feet in these. They're too big, but never mind."

"Thank you. It bothers me not to know who you are. I feel that I've known you a long time. What's your name?"

"Laure. My name is Laure Levancher. My husband was a professor at the Medical School in Lyons. When he died four years ago, I tried to live alone in our apartment until I realized that I'd soon go mad. In the end, I came here in order to rest for a couple of weeks. And here I stayed."

"My name is Betty."

"Enjoy your breakfast, Betty."

She tried to smile.

"I'm not too sure how hungry I really am. I thought I was hungry, but now . . ."

"Eat something all the same. My husband wouldn't have let you eat anything today, but I know from experience that medicine . . ."

Betty overcame her distaste, but even the coffee didn't have that good flavor that she had expected.

"I was very drunk, wasn't I?"

"More than that, you were very ill."

"No! I know that I was blind drunk and that I made a spectacle of myself."

"You obviously don't know The Hole yet. They don't even notice things like that there!"

The waiter returned with the bottle of mineral water and Laure went to get a flask of whisky from her room.

"You'll be able to have some too fairly soon, provided that your pulse doesn't start galloping again."

"Was it fast?"

"A hundred and forty-three."

She smiled as she mentioned the figure, as though she regarded it as irrelevant. She had said her name simply, without any vanity, more out of politeness than anything else, in order to put the young woman at her ease. She had told her why she was there and had explained as discreetly as possible why she needed to drink. On the other hand, she hadn't asked Betty her surname or any other questions about herself.

Betty had a strange intuition. She could have sworn that it wasn't from lack of curiosity that Laure behaved like that, but because she knew. Not the details, of course, for she couldn't know about her particular situation. But nevertheless she had understood.

And she didn't coddle her, pity her, or try to encourage her.

"If my cigarette disturbs you . . ."

"It doesn't bother me at all."

"Aren't you having anything else to eat?"

"I can't swallow another bite."

"Don't you want me to leave you on your own for a moment, to make a telephone call or write a letter?"

"No."

"You don't want to collect your things?"

What made her think that? She didn't say "luggage" but "things," as though she had guessed that Betty's apparent homelessness was definite.

"I'll leave you to yourself, now."

Betty cried out, almost shouting ;

"No!"

And at the same time she wondered whether she was going to be sick.

"Is anything wrong?"

"Yes."

"Feeling sick?"

"Yes."

"If you're like me, a drop of liquor will put you on your feet again. Have you ever tried that?"

She nodded.

"Do you want some?"

Laure gave her what remained of her whisky. Betty swallowed it in one gulp and felt she was going to vomit. She sat motionless, tense, ready to dash into the bathroom, until a wave of heat spread through her body and she finally relaxed.

"Feeling better?"

She heaved a long sigh.

"Whew! I thought I wouldn't even make it to the bathroom."

"Do you know where we are?"

"At Versailles. At the Carlton."

Laure didn't ask her how she knew or what else knew.

"Do you want to stay here a few days and rest?"

"I don't want to do anything."

It was true. Betty didn't ask herself any questions. Before her there was a void. There was no reason why she should be here rather than anywhere else.

"Listen, Betty. Do you mind if I call you by your first name?"

She looked instinctively at her wedding ring, which she hadn't thought of removing.

"Call me Laure, like everyone else. At The Hole, incidentally, people mostly go by their first names and, at some point in the evening, they usually get pretty familiar with each other."

Did she say this in order to explain the intimate way in which Mario and she had spoken to each other as they carried Betty to her car? Was she trying to suggest that there was nothing between them?

Betty blushed about having had such a thought, about having once more recalled the scene on the bed, real or unreal, but so vivid in her mind.

"I'll be straight with you, so I'm straight with everybody. Last night I realized that you didn't know what to do with yourself and I brought you back here because you needed a bed. Don't say anything. Let me go on. For twenty-eight years I was a happy woman, a good provincial housewife for whom her husband and her home were the whole world. If I'd been lucky enough to have had children, I wouldn't be here now."

Betty had no idea how much whisky Laure had had that day. She spoke without excitement or self-indulgence, but with a tone of exaggerated conviction, just as Betty herself spoke after two or three whiskies.

"At the moment, I consider that my life is over and that I no longer exist. Unless I'm wrong about you, you know what I mean. I could have locked myself into my apartment and waited for the end with dignity.

"I tried. I drank a lot, more than I do here, and at one point I almost went out of my mind.

"What I do at the moment, how I live, what happens to me, no longer matters. Tourists come and go, couples take refuge in this hotel for a few days, old men and convalescents settle down here and go for short walks in the park every afternoon.

"I no longer bother with them. Some of them greet me when they notice me here after several months, either because they think they know me or because they think I'm on the staff.

"I hardly ever go down to the dining room, and when I have a drink at the bar, it's usually when no one else is there, in order to have a word with Henri.

"I put you in the room next to mine thinking you might need somebody to look after you."

"I did," Betty interrupted her shyly.

She felt like a schoolgirl in front of a new teacher.

"I'm not trying to influence you. If you have somewhere else to go, go ahead. If you want to stay another night, or a few days, or longer, don't think twice about it; and if you'd rather have another room . . ."

"No."

"This evening, like yesterday evening, and every other evening for that matter, I'll go to The Hole."

A suspicion crossed Betty's mind: wasn't Laure saying these things in order to stop her thinking about her own problems? Ever since she had given her an injection, she had become a sort of doctor in Betty's eyes, and doctors sometimes play tricks like this on their patients.

"Was that the first time you've been there?"

"Yes."

"Did anything strike you about it?"

"I was in such a state!"

She didn't dare ask for another drink, although she wanted one. The effect of the last sip of whisky had passed and she needed another fillip.

"When Mario talks about his patrons, he likes to imply that they're all cracked; and he's not far wrong. Shall I tell you the story of Mario and The Hole?"

She said yes, still thinking about the drink that she wanted to deserve. Laure obviously thought about it, too.

"Do you need one?"

"I guess so."

"At once?"

"Would it be bad for me?"

Laure poured it out for her.

"You may have noticed that Mario likes to play it tough. A lot of his regular customers think he's been to prison several times. This idea excites them, the women.

"The truth is that he's worked as a waiter in a bar and then as a taxi driver in Toulon. You mustn't tell him you know: he'd never forgive me. He likes to say he was a sailor, like all the gangsters on the Riviera.

"He looks like a brute while in fact he's affectionate and, strange though it may seem, even rather shy.

"One day in Toulon, many years ago, he gave a ride in his taxi to a South American woman whose husband, a rich Columbian planter, had just died of a stroke in Monte Carlo.

"Was she as crazy as Mario claims? At all events, she took him on as her chauffeur and factotum and, for over a year, they drove her Rolls Royce all over the place, from Cannes to Deauville, from Paris to Biarritz, Venice and Mègeve. Am I boring you?"

"On the contrary."

Betty still saw the two bodies on the bed, and she was now sure that she hadn't been dreaming. But wasn't this room with pale blue paneling and the bust of Marie Antoinette on the mantelpiece, as well as the monotonous sound of the rain on the ever darker leaves outside, all a dream?

It was getting dark, The lamps, behind their little shades of pleated silk, were becoming brighter and brighter, and Betty pulled the damp bathrobe still closer around her naked body.

The dark woman in front of her was too large even when she was sitting down: she knew she was ungainly and didn't try to hide the fact. She smoked one cigarette after another, occasionally sipped at her drink, and played with one of her slippers on the tip of her toes.

If there were any other guests in the hotel, or any

members of the staff walking down the corridors, they couldn't be heard.

"As for the rest of the story, there is obviously a gap somewhere between what really happened and what is generally told, and I can't vouch for which is which. The Columbian woman was called Maria Urruti and appears to have come from one of the oldest families in her country. Ever since her husband's death, her family had been urging her to return home. They pursued her with letters and cables and threatened to stop her money, until, one fine day, she simply had to go back.

"'They're going to kill me!' she told Mario. 'They hate me. They want me to go back so that they can kill me or shut me up in a lunatic asylum. You must come with me, Mario, you who are so strong, and keep them from hurting me.'

"They left together, by boat because she was afraid of airplanes. Her family lived in a town called Cali at the foot of the Andes, on the Pacific coast, and in order to get there, they had to disembark at Buenaventura."

Betty gazed at the tree tops which were gradually being drowned in mist and started staring at a distant light between the branches which looked like a star. She wasn't thinking. She wasn't listening. The words flowed into her smoothly, like running water.

"Mario didn't have the chance to use force. Hardly had the boat docked than several black-haired men, Maria Urritu's relatives, rushed on board along with some policemen, and Maria was whisked away while the other passengers were still waiting to disembark.

"As for Mario, he left the boat a little later and found himself with no money whatsoever on an unknown wharf.

"He claims to have done every sort of job and implies that some of them were eminently illegal. He'll show you his scar, by the corner of his eye, which you may not have noticed.

"It's as well to pretend to believe him. I, for one, wouldn't be surprised if Maria's family hadn't given him a large sum of money in order to get rid of him.

"He spent some time in Venezuela, Panama, and Cuba. When he came back to France, he decided to open a bar near the S.H.A.P.E. headquarters for the benefit of American officers.

"That's The Hole, which you saw. With a few rare exceptions, the Americans have never gone there, either because they think it too close to their base or because they prefer Paris.

"To Mario's astonishment his clientele is made up of people he had never dreamed even existed, the people you saw last night, the 'crazies', as he calls them, foreigners or Frenchmen living between Versailles and Saint-Germain, near Marly, Louveciennes, and Bougival. Some come from still farther away, people with villas and large estates, often a wife and some children, who . . ."

She didn't finish the sentence but took her glass as though she wanted Betty to do the same.

"Crazies! Like me! People who've got nothing more . . ."

She started drinking without saying what she was going to say, and, not only because of the damp bathrobe, Betty shuddered.

3

"How do you like these cannelloni, Betty?"

Mario's voice was jolly, familiar, comforting.

"They're very good," she said, with a look of gratitude.

"You must admit that it's quite pleasant here."

"It's so pleasant that I already feel like an old *habituée*."

At the beginning of the evening, she had felt slightly

embarrassed: she was new here and she thought that everybody was looking at her and that they all remembered the incident of the night before. She got over her embarrassment very soon, however, especially when she realized that, thanks to Laure, who acted as a sort of guarantee, she had been adopted.

A mere detail confirmed this feeling. When, as occasionally happened, a regular patron exchanged a few words with Laure, he didn't even bother to lower his voice.

On the table, standing between them, was a huge dish of cannelloni and a flask of Chianti. The red wine was dark, almost black in the balloon-shaped glasses, with a pink, more luminous point in the middle. Outside, a cold wind plastered the rain onto the faces and clothes of the people getting out of their cars and, when they left, they always had some difficulty in moving out of the mud.

The barmaid with the big breasts was standing at her post, and there were more people at the bar than the evening before, but fewer seated in the cocktail lounge, maybe because it wasn't so late.

It was all just as she remembered it, even the red walls, covered with English prints of hunting scenes. Despite the state she had been in she had noticed everything the night before, and she was surprised to have proof of the fact.

One might have thought that she had been concerned exclusively with herself, with her own problems and her disgust. Besides, she had been so drunk that she had fallen off her chair. Everything had been spinning, in her life and around her, and yet she had taken an interest in such futile details as those postcards stuck in the frame of the mirror, behind the bottles on the bar. She was sure that one of them was of the bay of Naples and another of the temple of Angkor.

The room hardly seemed any larger to her today either. She saw that in fact there were two rooms and that the other one, where it also appeared possible to have dinner, was darker than the first and was illuminated solely by candles stuck into the bottles on the tables.

Was this section reserved for the initiated, for very old customers or for lovers? Did real lovers ever come to The Hole?

"How are you feeling?" inquired Laure.

"Fine for the time being."

She ate voraciously. She felt that her eyes were shining, her complexion was high and, at the slightest provocation, her lips spread into a faintly hesitant smile.

It was as though she were convalescing, and this was agreeable. She was perfectly aware that this feeling of well-being was temporary, superficial, that nothing had changed, that she was really in the same situation as before, with all the problems that she had accumulated and to which there was no solution.

Did Laure realize how fragile, how artificial her mood was? Did she know that from one moment to the next, it was going to start all over again, just as it had done the day before? She was being sustained by some liquor, by the fact of dining with somebody who was taking care of her. But she had experienced a similar feeling of relaxation the night before, too, as she sat opposite the doctor. It only took a glass or two.

There was no point in worrying about anything in advance. It was as though she were traveling, as though she were in another climate, in a new town, where one forgets about one's cares and one's own personality.

Laure knew her full name now. When they had gone down to the lobby, the receptionist had asked Betty:

"Would you be so kind as to fill in the card?"

And, when he read it, the man had said:

"Etamble, like the general?"

"I'm his daughter-in-law."

She had added:

"Is it possible to send for some luggage from Paris?"

"Have a word with the porter."

Laure had stood at a distance, discreetly. Betty told the man in uniform that there were a number of suitcases, perhaps even a trunk, to be fetched at 22 bis Avenue de Wagram.

"Do you know how many?"

"No."

"Do you think they'll fit into one car?"

"Probably. I'm almost sure."

"Maybe you should give me a note, just in case they refuse to hand them over."

She scribbled on a writing pad:

Please give my luggage to the bearer. Thank you.

This time she signed "Betty." It wasn't an official document. She didn't say anything else. There was nothing else to say.

"Shall I send for your things right now?"

"If you can, please."

"Will somebody be there?"

"There's always somebody ."

Somebody would have to be in the apartment, if only the nurse, because Anne-Marie was only nineteen months old.

She had gotten into Laurie's car which she remembered from the smell, from the rough texture of the upholstery. General Etamble had died the year before in Lyons where he had been living for some time. His wife was born in Lyons and came from the same social background as Laure, so the two women might well have met.

But Laure didn't mention it. Her behavior hadn't altered in any way. She was evidently capable of long silences, which were nevertheless not embarrassing, and then suddenly, for no apparent reason, she would launch into a long story.

"Do you recognize John?" she asked as they were eating, perhaps in order to stop Betty's mind wandering.

And since Betty didn't understand immediately:

"The English lord I mentioned to you yesterday. He's sitting to the left of the bar with a girl with fair hair in a leopard-skin coat."

She meant the bald man, tall and well built, with a slightly bloated face and a bushy mustache. He sat bolt upright on the bench like a retired army officer and gazed straight ahead, oblivious of his companion, who looked like a movie starlet.

Despite his high complexion and his blotchy cheeks, the Englishman had unmistakable distinction.

"He can go on like that without saying a word for two or three hours on end. He doesn't drink whisky, only brandy. Nobody knows what he thinks about while the liquor seeps into him little by little and he may not even know it himself.

"At some point, he'll get up and walk toward the door without a moment's hesitation. He can tell exactly how much he can take and nobody has ever seen him totter. The woman always follows him, the fair-haired girl today, another one tomorrow or next week, because he gets through with them quickly.

"His chauffeur is waiting for him outside in the Bentley. It's only a few minutes' drive to his estate at Louveciennes. He breeds Great Danes there.

"Jeanine, the barmaid with a hairy mole on her cheek, told me what happens next. She went there one night when he was alone, or rather, one night when his mistress had fallen ill and they had had to . . ."

She didn't bite her lip, but it came to the same thing.

"Like me yesterday," said Betty, quite gaily.

"She was in a far worse state and had to be taken to the hospital. Jeanine stood in for her, so to speak. From how she told it, I have reason to believe that the same performance takes place each time.

"To start with, in the hall, he gave her a drink, like a man of the world doing his duty as host. Then he took her to his room where he put on a dressing gown and sat in an armchair.

"He didn't say a word to Jeanine. She finally undressed while he remained seated and looked at her with apparent satisfaction, as if he were at the theater.

"He pointed to the bed and she lay down on it, waiting for something, anything, to happen. After a while, what with the silence in the room and in the whole house, she started to feel quite frightened.

"Still sitting in his armchair, he stared at her just as he is staring at the face opposite him at the moment. On a pedestal table, within his reach, stood a crystal decanter full of brandy. The only movement he made was to fill his glass, hold it in his palm in order to warm it, and occasionally sip at it.

"Jeanine thought she ought to try and make conversation. But when she saw him frown gloomily, she stopped.

"This lasted a long time, over an hour, and in the end she realized that John was asleep, his empty glass in his hand."

Laure didn't laugh, nor did Betty.

"They say he married one of the most beautiful women in England, who still lives in his house in London and his estate in Sussex. They aren't divorced;

they haven't quarreled. They're still on good terms and see each other now and again. He simply backed out, giving her her freedom, the day a war wound made him impotent. That was twenty years ago, and for twenty years, in the evening, he's been sitting in his armchair with a glass in his hand in front of a naked woman."

Betty didn't even dare turn toward the Englishman any more and Laure went on:

"A 'crazy', as our friend Mario would say."

At the bar, two women aged between thirty and forty, in trousers and sweaters, were eating one gherkin after another out of the same enormous jar. The Negro, Louis, appeared at almost regular intervals to show his beaming face as though he were performing an act in a variety show, and Betty began to wonder whether it wasn't all prearranged, whether it wasn't a put-up job, and whether the characters were authentic or not.

"What happened to Maria?" she asked suddenly.

This time it was Laure who didn't understand at first.

"Maria?"

Betty always asked questions like this. When she was a little girl, she used to make everybody laugh and one of the things she had said as a child had become proverbial in the house on Avenue de Versailles. It was before the war, at a time when her father was still alive.

"What happened to the frog?"

Her parents had read her a story about a frog and

other animals in a picture book. When the story was over, her little voice had broken the silence:

"What happened to the frog?"

Her father and mother had looked at each other without knowing what to say. In the book, the story was over. Normally there would have been no reason to take any further interest in the frog.

Subsequently, when she opened her mouth to ask a question, her father used to interrupt her, laughing: *"What happened to the frog?"*

Wasn't her question about the South American woman the same thing?

"Do you mean Maria Urruti?"

"Yes. I wonder if they locked her up."

"Mario has never heard from her since."

"How old was she?"

"About thirty. When he first told me about her, I assumed she must have been middle-aged, especially since her husband was almost seventy when he died in Monte Carlo."

Betty, too, was about thirty—or so one could say. She said nothing, went on eating her cheese, a brie, but without much enjoyment. She had to make an effort not to look around at the Englishman and, when she saw Jeanine laughing with the two women in trousers, she imagined her lying on the bed, a four-poster bed in her imagination, motionless and silent, under the immobile gaze of the man with his glass in his hand.

In Buenaventura, the family had boarded the boat, probably Maria's brothers, brothers-in-law, and cousins. She saw them as a compact, solid block. The authorities were on their side.

"How's it going?"

"Very well, Mario. We're eating."

"Great! There aren't many crazies here this evening. They must be afraid of getting wet."

He glanced at Betty as if to see how far gone she was, and then, before leaving them, he laid his hand on Laure's shoulder in an almost conjugal gesture.

"He's fond of his patrons really, and when they're not here he misses them."

In those few seconds, Betty had realized that she wasn't a "patron" to Mario and that, sooner or later, there would be something between them. Did Laure suspect it? Was she jealous? Was she satisfied with what he gave her?

Betty felt herself looking again for some form of support. She had started floating. She hadn't had that much to drink and she was determined to stop in time, for she didn't want to be ill again and make another spectacle of herself.

Yet she felt a slight regret for the previous night when she had sat there passively, with no worries, and nothing had mattered any more.

What mattered now? She had sent for her things. The receptionist of the Carlton must have dispatched a driver, perhaps even accompanied by a porter. Guy would have been in the drawing room with his mother, and probably with his brother and sister-in-law, too.

The two brothers, the two families, lived in the same

building. Guy was on the third floor, Antoine on the fourth. Antoine was the elder. He was thirty-eight and was in the army, just like his father. One day he too, would be a general. An artillery officer attached to the Ministry of Defense, his office was on Rue Saint-Dominique.

His wife, Marcelle, was the daughter of an officer and the sister of officers. They had two sons, Paul and Henri, who were at the *lycee.*

But if Antoine was the elder, why did they always go to Guy's apartment in the evening? Nobody had ever made a decision about this—it had simply happened like that.

Antoine sometimes came alone, in his smoking jacket, and joined Guy in his little study. On other occasions, Marcelle came with him and Betty had to keep her company.

There was a fireplace, with a log-fire in winter, and a large floor lamp with a shade of crinkly parchment. The children would be asleep, the two boys on the fourth floor, the girls on the third, and, at about ten o'clock, Elda, the nurse, a Swiss woman from Valais, would appear in the doorway to ask:

"May I go to bed, Madame?"

For people called Betty "Madame." She had a family, two children, a husband, a brother-in-law, a sister-in-law and, in Lyons, a mother-in-law who wrote to her sons every week and who came to Paris for a few days every two months or so.

When the general was still alive, he and Guy's

mother always used to go to the same hotel on the Left Bank. Since his death, Madame Etamble had taken to staying at the house on Avenue de Wagram, with her eldest son on the fourth floor.

Even if she didn't like Betty, she wasn't unpleasant to her; she simply looked at her as though she were trying to understand.

"Why she?" she seemed to be asking, and she would then glance at her son.

Betty used to ask herself the same question. Madame Etamble was right. Everybody was right, basically. Guy, too, and Betty was sure that he had loved her, that he still loved her, and that he was probably suffering a great deal.

She didn't have anything to hold against him. At the age of thirty-five, he had heavy responsibilities and serious worries, for almost since the time when he was a brilliant student at the Polytechnic Institute, he had held a key post at the National Mining Board on Boulevard Malesherbes, an impressive building resembling a fortress where national interests were at stake.

He was good-looking, better looking than Antoine, more delicate, as his mother would say, with fair hair and regular features. He was always dressed perfectly, not in dark suits like those worn by businessmen who are afraid of not being taken seriously, but usually in suits of light, muted colors, in supple, soft materials. He played tennis and he drove a sports car.

He was fairly cheerful by nature and could make Charlotte laugh for hours on end without ever running out of steam. When she was smaller, it had been he who put her to bed every evening, and he kept up the tradition with Anne-Marie.

Did Laure know the Etamble family?

Betty imagined them all in the drawing room that evening, when the driver gave them her note.

Where had they put her things? Who had taken her dresses out of the closet, collected all her underwear, her shoes, her various personal objects? Who had emptied the drawers of her dressing table and her little Louis XV desk?

Olga, the maid, who had always taken a still gloomier view of her than her mother-in-law, and who had big, masculine hands? Elda?

What suitcases had they used? She and her husband had never had separate suitcases of their own. They shared the luggage. Had they evaded the question by bringing down the large trunk from the attic?

She had been gone for three days, four now, and they had undoubtedly expected her to send for her things immediately, or the next morning at the latest, since she had left the house with nothing but what she was wearing.

Weren't they worried about not having heard from her? Did they fear that she had jumped into the Seine, or that she had swallowed a tube of sleeping pills?

If she rang the Carlton, she could find out whether

the driver had come back, whether they had given him the luggage, whom he had seen and what they had said to him.

Perhaps her mother-in-law had had a worse attack than usual. She had a weak heart, that was certain. She had been having medical attention because of it for a long time. Even if she occasionally exaggerated her condition in order to make people pity her, she was nonetheless ill and, when Antoine had come down, he had been very alarmed by the sight of his mother's violet lips.

"May I ask you what you're thinking about? Or am I being indiscreet?"

"My mother-in-law. You must know her."

"She lives three doors away from me, on Quai de Tilsitt. I have kept my apartment in Lyons and occasionally I go there on a pilgrimage, so as not to lose touch."

Touch with what? With her former life? With her friends? With her husband's memory? Although she didn't specify, Betty was almost sure that she had understood.

"I used to meet them quite frequently in the old days. I saw her and the general at ceremonies or official dinners which we had to attend. Apart from these obligations my husband and I saw very few people—doctors, a couple of lawyers, and a musician whom nobody has ever heard of."

Did they, too, have an upholstered drawing room, a floor lamp with parchment shade, a piano, and a sofa where the ladies sat next to each other? Was there a clock that ticked out the minutes more slowly than anywhere else and, outside, day and night, the roar of traffic which acted as a reminder of another life?

"She's in Paris," said Betty.

She didn't want to talk about it, but she could not stop herself. She led herself to believe that she would stop when she wanted, that she would go no further than she intended

"For three days," she added. "Four now! It's odd. I always count one day less."

Only she knew what she meant by that. For Laure it must have been a riddle.

"I married one of her sons, the youngest, Guy."

It was Laure who went on:

"The one who didn't go into the army, to the despair of the general."

"His brother Antoine is at the Ministry of Defense."

"And he married a Mademoiselle Fleury. I knew her older sister. Although the Fleurys are not from Lyons, they have some relatives there who are vaguely related to my family. As for Madame Etamble, she's a Gouvieux. Her father owned a factory of chemical products that his sons took over—all except for one, Hector, who's a doctor and who runs the ophthalmological department at the Broussais Hospital where my husband used to work."

She smiled, rather ironically.

"You see! I'm talking as I would in a drawing room in Lyons. I also know that the Etambles have an estate in Chassagne Forest near Chalamont, not far from where my brother-in-law goes duck shooting."

"I've been there."

"Often?"

"Every year for the past six years, since I was married. The whole family spends August there—Madame Etamble, the general when he was still alive, the two brothers, the wives and children . . ."

She didn't know why her eyes were swollen with tears. She had always hated August at Les Etangs, the huge house with its sham turrets, the floors that creaked, the iron beds they put up for the children, the damp mattresses, the spongy park.

She longed for the sea, a beach, the sun, salt water on her face, the freedom of a swimsuit. She longed for music in the cafés, shellfish and white wine, for a speedboat bouncing over the waves.

For hours on end, Guy would play tennis with his brother, or sometimes with the neighbors. On some days, the two women were asked to make a double's team and Betty would miss all her serves in her effort to play well.

"We made a mistake" she concluded by way of summary, and Laure fully understood.

"I realized that."

Laure turned to Joseph and made a sign. Betty noticed. She could have said no, but she didn't because that seemed the only solution.

She couldn't go on talking like that, coldly, like

relatives who meet each other and recall family memories. The image she had just conveyed was false, and Laure must have known it. It had everything to do with the family. The others didn't count. The others hadn't done anything.

"I've got two children," she said, staring into space.

Laure waited for her to continue, in silence.

"Last month Charlotte blew out the four candles on her birthday cake. Anne-Marie is nineteen months old and has started to really talk."

Joseph brought whisky and soda. Why didn't Laure stop him, why didn't she prevent her from drinking? Did she who knew so many things not realize that it might start all over again, that it was inevitably going to start all over again?

Did she do it on purpose, so that Betty should confide in her, because she needed to know people's secrets? She had said:

"Mario calls them his 'crazies'. You'll see!"

And hadn't she taken a certain pleasure in telling the story of Maria Urruti?

When she disclosed John's infirmity a minute ago, Betty had the impression that she was undressing him in public, that she was also undressing the barmaid with the big breasts, as well as the fair-haired starlet and all the other women who had followed the Englishman to his estate at Louveciennes. Betty was now ashamed to look at him.

Wasn't Laure going to do the same to her? Wouldn't

she tell the story of the little Etamble woman one day, as impassively, as impersonally as her husband used to describe a clinical case?

What had they said about her the night before, or, rather, at dawn, when Mario had come to join her in her room?

"Is she asleep?"

"I put her out with an injection."

"What was the matter with her? Did you undress her?"

Had Laure told him what her body was like? Had she added that she was dirty? Had they both come to look at her as she slept?

"Where do you think she comes from?"

"Bernard picked her up in a bar."

Maybe Laure had pointed out that her suit was made by one of the best designers in Paris and that her underthings had been bought on Rue Saint-Honoré. They might even have opened her handbag.

It would have been perfectly natural to open it, quite apart from any bad intentions or unhealthy curiosity. They had picked her up on the floor of The Hole like a sick animal. Nobody knew where she came from, not even the doctor who was pursuing imaginary rabbits in his room all the while.

Her pulse had been beating at a rate of a hundred and forty-three. An accident might have happened and neither Laure nor Mario would have known whom to alert except for the police.

Had they found the check? For a second she wondered whether it wasn't because of the check for a million francs that . . .

She didn't want to go on! She wasn't as exhausted as she had been the evening before. She had slept. Laure had looked after her. She had had a bath. She had become almost normal, like the four people who had just come in and who made everybody smile.

Betty smiled too, reluctantly, and yet they were perfectly normal, and if her father had come here with his family he would probably have behaved in the same way.

The man could have been almost anything, an industrialist, a lawyer, a civil servant, a general practitioner: a middle-aged man, at his ease, self-assured, not obviously naive.

It wasn't his fault if his wife had grown so fat and if her complexion was as pink as a piece of candy. In any other place, she would simply have appeared as the mother of a family, with nothing ridiculous about her.

Of course, there were the twins, two tall girls of seventeen or eighteen, as fat and as pink as their mother, and both dressed in green, identical from head to toe.

All four were hungry. They had come a long way and were delighted to have discovered a restaurant in the country.

When he came in, however, the father had frowned as he noticed Jeanine at the bar and he had had to maneuver past the two women in trousers so as not to brush against them.

The next moment, he saw the beaming face of the Negro Louis, who appeared and disappeared like a figure at a puppet show.

He let his wife and daughters sit down, sat down himself, and clapping his hands, called:

"Waiter!"

Joseph approached in a leisurely manner.

"Whisky?"

"No, thanks."

He turned to the women.

"Would you like an apéritif?"

They said no, as expected.

"Give me the menu."

"There is no menu, sir."

He looked curiously at the tables where people were eating.

"It is a restaurant, isn't it?"

"Yes, indeed."

Mario intervened.

"Good evening, sir, good evening, ladies. I suppose you'll have the cannelloni?"

"What else have you got?"

"Some cheese; marvelous brie; some salad, and *riz à l'impératrice.*"

"I mean as a main dish."

"Cannelloni."

Laure's foot brushed against Betty's under the table and Betty had to smile. The man looked around in slight alarm at the walls, at the bar, at Jeanine once again, and finally his eyes met John's fixed stare.

"Will you have the cannelloni?"

"Why not."

The doctor had come in and had diverted Betty's attention. He was dressed as meticulously as the day before, still in gray, and he walked rather stiffly. He had recognized her at once and, after a moment's hesitation, had come forward.

"Good evening, Laure."

Then he bent over and kissed Betty's hand.

"I hope you've forgiven me for leaving you last night, in as much as I did leave you? Laure must have told you. . . ."

After bowing once more, he went to sit on a stool at the bar.

The four newcomers had resigned themselves to having cannelloni and the Chianti that had been placed authoritatively on their table. They appeared ill at ease and, as if to reassure themselves, were conversing loudly.

"Was Auntie surprised to see you both arrive so unexpectedly?"

"Will you believe it, Daddy," said one of the girls in the tone of an amateur dramatic-club hopeful, "Auntie was up in the attic, going through some boxes. You remember the attic and all that weird stuff up there?"

She was playing to the gallery and John's stare, fixed on her, seemed to excite her.

"We went up without making any noise, then

Laurence did one of her moos. It sounded just like a cow had climbed up to the attic, and Auntie dropped the pile of books she was holding. . . ."

If Guy had arrived here without being warned, wouldn't he, too, have felt ill at ease? Antoine certainly would. And Marcelle! But Antoine and Marcelle wouldn't have hesitated to turn on their heels and walk out again. Hadn't Betty herself ended up by shouting the evening before?

She wouldn't shout again. She was no longer scared. Nevertheless, she did feel a slight sense of distress as she examined the faces around her.

She suspected that Laure had other stories to tell her, that in a few days' time, in a few hours' time, the characters who had hitherto been anonymous would become as vivid as the doctor, the Englishman, and that Maria Urruti whom she couldn't get out of her mind.

"What happened to the frog?"

One day, somebody might even ask, with compassion mixed with curiosity:

"What ever became of little Betty?"

She always came back to herself. Because in the final analysis, at the very bottom, there was a "little Betty" who was struggling to understand herself, who wanted other people to make an effort to understand her.

Nor was it out of endearment that she referred to herself as "little." She was in fact small, fragile, delicate; she had never weighed more than ninety pounds.

Only when she was pregnant had she put on some weight, but so little that the doctors had been quite worried, especially the second time, and had thought of trying to make her give birth after seven months.

Did the fact that she felt smaller and weaker than others have some influence on her behavior? Someone had told her so, a medical student who had played at psychoanalyzing her for a while.

She had believed him at the time. She had also believed that she loved him. She had tried to answer his questions with the utmost sincerity, until she realized that his questions were only concerned with one single subject and were only intended for a single purpose.

She hadn't broken with him immediately. She had gone on with the game because it had excited her, too. It was he who had grown tired of it before she had, probably thinking that she lacked imagination and didn't vary her answers enough. He hadn't even said good-by to her. He had just disappeared.

The four newcomers were eating. The fair-haired girl was waiting. The Negro occasionally showed his face in the chink of a door.

Bernard walked toward the lavatory with great dignity, and Mario followed him with his eyes. Laure drank in little sips, watching Betty over her glass.

"It's not their fault," sighed Betty, hopelessly.

She wasn't referring to the table with the twins but to the Etamble family, the mother, the two sons, the sister-in-law, the elder brother's sons, and her own daughters. Her two daughters who were no longer hers!

She had to come back to it. It was inevitable. She had to talk and, in order to talk as much as she needed she had to drink.

But not here. She didn't want to make another spectacle of herself, to see those faces turn toward her as they were turned toward the four newcomers, those eyes focused on her as they had been the night before.

She emptied her glass in one gulp and said nervously:

"Would you mind very much if we left?"

"Do you feel sick?"

She didn't feel sick, but it was better not to admit it.

"I don't know. I'd rather go home."

She had said *go home,* as if the room with blue paneling and the bust of Marie Antoinette were already her home.

4

"Your luggage has arrived, Madame Etamble. I sent it up to your room."

"I don't suppose there was a message?"

"The driver didn't say anything about that. He just gave me this for you."

Seeing the envelope from a distance, she felt a thrill

as though she were expecting something; but in fact she wasn't expecting anything, wasn't even hoping for anything from that quarter. She was humiliated by her reaction, especially because the porter, who had carried her, blind drunk, to her room the night before, now, probably out of irony, spoke to her with exaggerated respect.

As she should have guessed, the envelope contained only the keys of the suitcases. No note. Why would anyone have written to her? The address was in Elda's handwriting.

When Betty opened the door of room 53 a little later, and the two women saw three large suitcases and some parcels in the middle of the room, Laure turned toward the adjoining room, murmuring:

"I'll leave you to yourself. I'll see you later."

"Do you want to go back to The Hole?"

"No, but I suppose you want to unpack in peace."

"Would you mind staying with me?"

"Of course not. I didn't want to disturb you. I've always loved packing and unpacking, though I've never really moved anywhere; when my husband was still alive, the only journeys I ever made were to accompany him to an occasional medical congress."

There was a large, soft parcel at the foot of the bed and Betty immediately tore open the blue paper.

"My mink!"

She couldn't conceal her joy, for she wasn't sure that they would send her her mink coat. Her sister-in-law Marcelle didn't have one, although she was older, and had to make do with an astrakhan coat. When Guy mentioned a mink to her two years earlier, he had explained:

"It's not a present so much as an investment. In our position, you'll need a mink sooner or later. The longer I wait before I buy you one, the more expensive it will be. Since it lasts a lifetime . . ."

Consequently he could have regarded it less as her personal garment than as capital, family property. He had sent it to her all the same and, if Laure hadn't been there, she would have put it on at once for the mere pleasure of being wrapped in it, for the reassuring sensation of luxury it gave her.

"Is it wild mink?"

"It was guaranteed."

"I was stupid enough to get a ranch-mink coat, and after a few years, it looked like rabbit. Shall I pour you a drink?"

Betty suddenly became excessively polite.

"You're always treating me."

"I promise to let you buy the next bottle, the next two bottles, if you like. I'll even show you where I get them."

Betty tried the keys in the locks, opened the cases, then the closet and the bureau. Laure came back with two glasses just as she was opening the last case, the smallest, a blue leather bag which she usually used for her toilet articles.

On the top of the case, well in evidence, were two photographs, one of Charlotte on her fourth birthday and one of Anne-Marie clinging to her parents' bed, taken on the Sunday when she had first walked.

Guy, in his pajamas, had run to get his camera. In a corner, one could just see the edge of the striped apron of the nurse who stood there ready to catch Anne-Marie if she fell.

"My daughters . . ." she murmured, pointing to the photographs.

"The elder one looks like you. She has your eyes. She'll be very engaging."

Laure looked at her out of the corner of her eye, thinking she was moved, perhaps even expecting her to burst into tears. But Betty was perfectly calm, far cooler than when she had seen the envelope downstairs or when she had spotted the suitcases from the doorway. If she grabbed the glass of whisky that Laure had poured out for her, it wasn't in order to gain courage.

"Here's to you and to all you've done for me."

It was as though she had started to behave conventionally now that she had recovered her belongings. Admittedly, there was a note of irony in her voice, of irony that was addressed to herself, not to Laure. As she picked up the photographs and threw them onto the bed she said:

"Anyway, they're not my children any more, and I wonder if they ever were mine, after the time they were inside me. . . ."

In a sudden flurry of activity she seized heaps of underwear which she placed in the drawers, came back to the suitcases, returned to the bureau, to the closet, and continued to talk, her voice clear, her features tense, without even bothering to look at Laure or attempting to judge her reactions.

"Do you believe in motherly love?"

She expected the silence that followed her question and she went on:

"I forgot that you didn't have any children. So you can't know. I mean the sort of motherly love they write about in books, talk about at school and sing about. When I got married, I imagined that I would have children one day and I liked the idea. It was part of everything: the family, the home, holidays at the beach. Then, when I was told I was pregnant, I was confused by the fact that it had all happened so quickly, that I had barely had time to grow up.

"I had been married to my husband for less than two years, yet suddenly the family no longer seemed concerned for me but only for the child that was about to be born. Or if they did concern themselves about me, it was only in connection with the baby, and the baby always came first. Even before I gave birth, I had become the mother.

"You'll think that I was jealous. It's almost true. Not altogether, though. I had just started living. I had looked forward to so many things the day when I would at last have a man of my own!

"My idea of marriage was to be just the two of us, but there were three of us almost immediately.

"I didn't think like that every day, of course. There

were times when I was touched by it, especially when I felt the baby moving inside me. Shortly afterward, my health started to worry them—not because of me but because of the baby—and I had to look after myself, to spend most of my time in bed.

"In the evening, my husband would come and sit next to me for half an hour, three quarters of an hour, and then, when he had nothing else to say to me, he would go back to his study, or to see Antoine and his wife in the drawing room.

"He brought me flowers. Everybody brought me flowers, everybody was kind to me, even the maid, Olga, who had been working for Guy before I arrived in the house and who always regarded me as an intruder.

"My mother-in-law was pleased with me, too.

"'Good girl! Think about your baby, your responsibility, and obey the doctor's orders.'

"They all watched me surreptitiously to make sure that I never broke the rules. I was so fragile, you see!

"Wasn't it natural that they should have worried about the future Etamble? Since Antoine, the eldest, had two sons, it never crossed anybody's mind that Guy wouldn't have a son, too."

She walked to and fro while Laure helped her by putting her dresses on hangers. Since there weren't enough of them in the closet, she went to get more from her own room.

"I was taken to hospital too soon and I had to wait

forty-eight hours. I was scared. I was sure I was going to pay for everything. Even now I can't explain what I meant by that. It was a vague idea of justice, of a justice which I didn't even recognize. By giving life to somebody else, I would pay in one way or another, either by suffering, or with my own life, or by being paralyzed for the rest of my life."

"I understand."

Betty was surprised and frowned.

"I never thought that anyone else could understand that and I never mentioned it to anyone for fear of being laughed at. The child was born, a girl. The family pretended to be happy, especially my husband, who never looked at me as affectionately as he did that day.

"At the time I was delighted. Then I began to understand that that affection wasn't meant for me, but for the mother of his child.

"Because it was *his* child. Any woman could have taken my place and given him one more easily than I did, without all the miseries and worries of those last months. And who knows? Another woman might even have given him the son he wanted so badly.

"The nurse, who had been engaged from a Swiss school, was at the hospital at the same time as myself, ready to take over the baby.

"Get some rest, darling. Elda is there to look after the child.

"With my tiny breasts, there was no question of

feeding the child. The doctors, the nurses, the family, everybody came in and out on tiptoe, and only stayed for a second in my room.

" 'Get some rest!'

"And I heard them whispering and laughing next door.

"I'm not looking for excuses. I'm trying to understand. The result might have been the same even if it had gone differently. I'm not a monster. I should imagine exactly the same thing happens to thousands of other women.

"I never felt the call of blood, the call of the flesh. I was shown a tiny being whom I didn't even know how to hold properly, and the nurse immediately took her away again as if to put her somewhere safe.

"I went several times a day into the nursery in our house on Avenue de Wagram, and I went with the best will in the world. Either the child was asleep and Elda put a finger to her lips, or she was being fed and I was told not to disturb her, or she was having diapers changed and all I could do was to watch.

"Everything was clean and tidy. In the kitchen and in the apartment, too, thanks to Olga, who didn't need me to look after the house.

"That was four years ago. Charlotte has learned how to walk and how to speak; she's growing up, but she's still not my daughter.

"I don't know what they'll tell her: either that I'm dead or that I've gone on a long journey."

"Won't you ever see her again?"

She shook her head so violently that her hair fell into her face.

"They don't want me to," she said, almost in a whisper.

Then, delving into her suitcase:

"I promised."

She stood up again, a large yellow envelope in her hand.

"Don't let's talk about it. Where's my glass?"

"Here."

"Thanks. If I go on, I'll end up by making you miserable, too. It was Elda who packed my belongings, I can tell from the way she did it. She thought she was pleasing me by putting in the children's photographs and, who knows, she may be right. That belongs to my past, too, like this envelope full of old photographs. I'd forgotten all about it. I wonder where she found it."

She was talking volubly and, although all the lights were on, she thought it was dark in the room. Dark and damp.

"One day, when I was about twenty, I bought an album to stick these photographs into. I hoped they would constitute a sort of life history.

"There! I can see the album jutting out under my dressing case. I never stuck anything into it. It has remained just as it was when I bought it at the stationer's, and yet I had plenty of time. If I'd had less time . . ."

She shook herself again. Her voice changed key.

"Do you want to see my father? I only saw him until I was eight years old because war broke out, the Germans invaded, and as soon as food supplies were scarce, I was sent to stay with an aunt in Vendée. My parents said I wasn't very strong. In Vendée one got all the food one wanted, butter, eggs, meat, and even real white bread.

"Here! This is my father. Just as I always remember him. He was too proud of his dirty coveralls ever to agree to be photographed in a Sunday suit. His hair was always on end.

"'Do comb your hair,' my mother used to sigh in embarrassment.

"'Why should I? Do you want me to leave a false image of myself?'

"He loved jokes and made fun of his customers. At dinner he used to imitate them to make me laugh and he was able to mimic all their voices perfectly.

"I've no idea what he did during the occupation. My mother swore that she didn't know either. It was only much later, when he was awarded a posthumous decoration and there was talk of a pension, that she mentioned his mysterious activities.

"I don't think he was ever in any of the Resistance groups because he was a sort of anarchist who didn't believe in anything and poked fun as much at Pétain as at De Gaulle, as much at Americans and Russians as at the Germans.

"The Gestapo came for him all the same, a few weeks before the liberation of Paris. We didn't hear anything more about him until two years later when my mother was informed officially that he had been shot.

"Nobody knows exactly where. Not in a camp or a prison but, according to some evidence, on a station platform where a batch of prisoners on their way to Germany were taken off the train."

Holding out a photograph taken in front of the pearl-gray curtain of a photographer's studio, she said, coldly:

"My mother."

"Don't you ever see her?"

"From time to time. Rarely. Once my father had disappeared she ran the business herself for a few months, then she took on a chemist to whom she made the whole thing over two years ago, keeping only part of the apartment on the first floor for herself."

"Didn't she marry again?"

Betty looked surprised, shocked. Surely her mother was an old woman. Then she suddenly realized that her mother had become a widow when she was only forty, at a far younger age than Laure.

"Me, about twelve weeks old."

The traditional photograph of a baby sprawling on a bear skin.

"The only time in my life I've ever been chubby."

"You're not thin."

After all, Laure had seen her naked.

"Not too thin. Not as thin as I look when I'm dressed."

She smiled slightly, in spite of everything.

"Me again, when I was four years old and went to the kindergarten. And here I was eight, the day before I left for La Pommeraye. My mother accompanied me and, trains being what they were just then, it was quite an expedition."

She passed over the aunts and uncles in silence, old glossy photographs mounted on cardboard.

"Do you know Vendée?"

"Not well. Only Luçon, Les Sables d'Olonne, La Roche-sur-Yon, too, where I spent the night in a hotel overlooking a huge square."

"I've never been there. La Pommeraye is on the other side of the province, in the Bocage, near the border of Deux-Sèvres. The Sèvre Niortaise crosses the village which is so small and so remote that hardly any Germans were seen there during the whole of the war.

"My uncle François, who married my mother's sister Rachèle, was the bigwig there, not only because he owns the only inn, but because he also sold grain, fertilizer, and cattle.

"I haven't got a photograph of him. He was an enormous man with a walrus mustache, small, cunning, rather wicked eyes, velvet breeches and, all the year around, from dawn to dusk, leather gaiters.

"I remember his smell, the smell of the inn, the good musty smell in the rooms, and the feather beds one could sink into. . . ."

She was holding a photograph which seemed to surprise her and change her trend of thought.

"I'd forgotten that I had a picture of Thérèse."

She showed it to Laure without letting it go, still looking at it herself with a certain excitement.

"The smallest one on the left is me, aged eleven. Look at my thin legs and straight braids! My aunt always hurt me when she braided my hair. . . ."

From the faded, blurred photograph two little girls looked out: they were standing very stiffly in front of the stone steps of a village church.

"Who is Thérèse?"

"She was the maid at the inn. She came from a state orphanage.

"She can't have been much over fifteen at the time and always wore the same black dress, the only one she had, which emphasized excessively the shape of her pointed little breasts. When I was ten, I was already impressed by them, and I would have given anything to have them myself.

"Thérèse served in the dining room when my aunt was busy. She made the beds, too, peeled the vegetables, and often went to get the two cows in the field.

"She never complained. She didn't laugh either. My aunt, who thought she was sly, was at her all day long, calling in her high-pitched voice:

"'Thérèse! . . . Thé-rè-se! . . .'

"'Yes, Ma'm,' Therese would murmur, suddenly appearing next to her when everybody thought she was somewhere else.

"I would have liked to have been her friend, but she

was too old for me, so I simply hung around her. I'd heard someone say she was a waif and this word seemed magical to me. It made me think of Thérèse as somebody extraordinary, whom I envied in spite of my love for my father. . . ."

She took her glass and dropped into an armchair, the yellow envelope on her knees with the little photograph on top of it. She continued to look at it from time to time.

"Schwartz used to badger me about her the whole time! Schwartz was the medical student I told you about. He used to wash dishes in a bar in the evenings in order to pay for his studies, and he lived in a servant's room near Place des Ternes. That was how I met him, because he lived almost next door to us."

She went on with a note of defiance:

"I was married, of course. I'd even had Charlotte. A year before. Or almost. When I lay on his bed, I could see hundreds of rooftops and smoking chimneys."

Laure didn't flinch.

"After he'd gone on questioning me about subjects which you can guess, I finally told him about Thérèse. He claimed that this incident had a deeper effect on me than all the rest of my childhood. He made me repeat the story so often that I became quite obsessed with it."

"What happened with Thérèse?"

"You can well imagine that when I was eleven I knew as much as most girls of my age, if not more. I lived in the country; I'd seen the animals. In the pasture near the inn was the breeding bull that covered all the cows in the locality, and we always used to pass that field on our way from school.

"I'd seen boys, too. Unlike many of my schoolmates, however, I had always refused to touch them.

"Every Saturday, my aunt drove her cart to the market at Saint-Mesmin, the next village, to sell her chickens, ducks, and her cheese, for she used to make pot cheese with skimmed milk.

"There, and everywhere else in the country, I suppose, the men look after the cattle while the women look after the poultry, butter, and cheese.

"Were we on holiday? Or had I skipped school for some reason I can't remember?

"I can still see myself alone in the courtyard, in the garden, then in the square in front of the church. It was as though the village was empty, probably because of the market at Saint-Mesmin.

"The priest went by and waved to me. It was summer. It was hot. One could see the gravel on the river bed, and the water dividing into thin streams.

"At one point I went back to the inn, and there was no one there either. The door of the cellar was half open. I went up to it in order to close it. But first I looked into the semi-darkness which always intrigued me, and, just behind the door, I saw my uncle standing there. He was covering Thérèse, who had arched forward with her head against the whitewashed wall.

"I say 'covering'; it was the only word I knew at the time, the word that everybody in the village used.

"I didn't budge. It didn't occur to me to leave. I was hypnotized by Thérèse's thin white thighs which my uncle penetrated with brutal thrusts.

"He'd seen me, he knew I was there, but he didn't stop and, breathing very heavily, he said:

"'You, little girl, if you ever dare mention it to your aunt, I'll do the same to you!'

"I still didn't run away. I moved back slowly, leaving the cellar door wide open, still staring at them in fascination.

"I would have liked to have stayed until the end, to have seen Thérèse's face and to have heard her voice.

"In my eyes, she had become more extraordinary than ever. She didn't cry, didn't struggle. Her features were hidden by her hair and her folded arm, but I can still see her black stockings which stopped above her knees, her black dress tucked up over her shoulders, and her pants on the ground, around her feet.

"I didn't dare wait until the end for fear that my uncle might change his mind and immediately carry out his threat, for fear that he would hurt me.

"I kept out of his way until the evening, and as you can well imagine I didn't breathe a word to my aunt.

"I realized subsequently that she suspected the truth but preferred to ignore it.

"I hung around Thérèse more and more, without ever having the courage to ask her any questions. I suppose that what worried me most was the fact that she was halfway between being a little girl, like me, and being an adult.

"I had never really regarded her as an adult, and on

several occasions she had asked me if she could play with the doll my mother had sent me from Paris.

"Schwartz told me a great many things about what I felt for Thérèse, some may have been true, but others were probably exaggerated.

"He said that I envied her, and that's quite true. Even if I didn't admit it at the time, I now realize that I did feel envious.

"When I started trailing her, I realized that she didn't only do things like that with my uncle but that she did them with other men, too, and that my uncle was jealous.

"He watched her and, when she was alone with the guests in the inn, he would suddenly appear, having arrived from a shed or from the stables, and stand near the counter, with a distrustful look in his eye.

"Once in the winter, after supper, when it was already dark, I saw her lying in the grass at the edge of the road, between the inn and the grocer's, where she had been sent to buy something.

"The man was a farmhand whom I recognized from his red rubber boots, because he was the only one with boots that color.

"On another occasion I went past the room where a young traveling salesman was staying. The door was closed. I didn't see anything, but I heard Thérèse saying:

" 'Hurry up. If I stay too long, he'll come upstairs.'

"Judging from the noises I heard, they were either lying on the bed or sitting on the edge of it.

"So, at the age of fifteen, Thérèse was no longer a

child, like me and my friends. She was a woman. For in my eyes to be a woman was just that. I didn't think she could enjoy it and, according to Schwartz, that was what marked me.

"In other words, to be a woman was to be submissive, to be a victim, and for me that had something pathetic about it.

"Do you think I'm ridiculous? Am I boring you?"

"On the contrary."

Betty thought that Laure's features were a little blurred, and she let her fill their glasses again and return to her armchair before she went on:

"That's about all there is to tell. My uncle never touched me, despite his threat and despite the fact that I stayed at La Pommeraye until I was fourteen.

"Since food supplies were still scarce in Paris immediately after the war, and since my mother had so much to do once my father was gone, she decided to leave me there a little longer.

"What would I have done if my uncle had dragged me behind the cellar door? I would certainly have been terrified. I don't know if I would have screamed and, quite frankly, I don't think I would have struggled.

"I'm going to go still further, and I may even shock you if you're a Catholic."

"I'm not."

"Nor am I. My parents weren't either, my father less than anyone. Only my aunt went to mass and it was she who made me take my first communion without my parents knowing about it.

"I was twelve. It was after the incident of Thérèse in the cellar. When I went to confession, I didn't say a word to the priest about my uncle or what I'd seen, but I muttered something about frequently having evil desires.

"I felt it was wrong and, at the same time, I had the impression that what happened to Thérèse was a little like receiving a sacrament.

"A punishment, too, so that when I gave birth I vaguely felt that I was paying for something.

"To my mind, women were made for that. For men to humiliate them and hurt them in their body.

"I was longing to be hurt in my body, to receive this consecration, and I used to examine my breasts in despair, because they wouldn't grow. I used to look at my skinny legs in the mirror, as straight as sticks, and my narrow, round, childish belly."

Without knowing it, she had assumed the same fixed smile as in the photograph taken at La Pommeraye. Laure was grave. The radiators were turned on, yet both of them felt that the room was growing cold.

"Everything I've done since, I've done because I wanted to do it. That's what I wanted to tell you, out of honesty, because I've always wanted to be honest. I'm not a victim. I'm not to be pitied. Nobody ever hurt me. If anything, I hurt others.

"That was obviously why Schwartz left me without a word, simply by changing his address and neighborhood from one day to the next.

"I suppose he felt I was dragging him God knows where.

"As for Guy, he's thirty-five, with no wife and with two daughters who are going to grow up and be quite a burden for him one day, unless he marries again.

"Ah! I've just remembered a word which conveys almost everything I'm trying to explain. As I moved slowly, reluctantly, away from that cellar door, do you know why I so much wanted to wait for Thérèse and talk to her? To ask her:

"'Show me your wound.'

"The word has just come back to me after so many years. I wanted to have a wound too. All my life I . . ."

She looked Laure in the eyes, with an unpleasant expression, and ended harshly:

"All my life, I've been running after my wound."

She had sworn to herself that she wouldn't start crying again. But it wasn't possible. Thick tears burst out from under her eyelids, ran down her nose, put a salty taste into her mouth. At the same time she was laughing.

"I'm idiotic, aren't I? Say I'm an idiot! I've spoiled everything, wrecked everything, dirtied everything. I've spent my time dirtying myself, and I'm telling you all this in order to be pitied. All my life, ever since the age of fifteen, yes, fifteen, in order to copy Thérèse, I've been nothing but a whore. A whore, do you hear?"

She leapt up, incapable of remaining seated, and started pacing the room while Laure didn't budge from her armchair.

"It isn't because my husband kicked me out or

because the Etamble family kept me out of the clan that I started drinking. It's not because I sold my children, either. I know the words by heart:

"*The undersigned, Elisabeth Etamble, born Fayet . . .*

"Because I had to put my full first name. It was an official document. Elisabeth Etamble, born Fayet, admits that she's a whore, that she's always had lovers, before and after her marriage, that she picked them up in bars like a pro, that she took them home and that she was found making love almost next door to her children's room. . . .

"And now, my eyes full of tears, I'm telling you about my memories, my childhood memories!

"Look! When I say I sold them, I'm telling the truth. . . ."

She grabbed her handbag, fumbled in it frantically, threw the check onto Laure's knees.

"A million francs. On account, of course, because it alone would be too cheap.

"'I don't want you to end up in the street,' he told me.

"'He' is Guy, you see? Upright Guy, kindhearted Guy, General Etambles's son who had the misfortune to fall in love with a girl and marry her without looking into her past, as his mother advised him.

"It was Guy who dictated, and the others were all there listening, to make sure that he didn't leave anything out; Antoine, Marcelle in a dressing gown, who had been dragged out of bed for the occasion, and the general's widow, who held her left side with both hands, waiting for the doctor.

"She may have died of it.

"'Give me your address as soon as you have one so that my lawyer can get in touch with you. I'll make sure that you have everything you need, whatever happens.'

"And that's what happened to my wound, to all my wounds, my hundreds of wounds, wounds made by all the men I've chased after in order to punish myself."

She grabbed the bottle with a swift movement, as though she were afraid Laure was going to prevent her, and raised it to her lips in a deliberately dissolute gesture.

"I've been drinking for years, on the sly, because I couldn't live without it, because I can't be like them and, anyhow, I wouldn't want to be. I stopped drinking when I was expecting Charlotte, and then Anne-Marie, because the doctor told me it could harm them.

"I was quite prepared to give birth to the children of a whore, since my husband was so anxious that I should. But I had enough pride left not to give birth to children who would be ill or deformed through any fault of mine.

"Well, when I went to hospital, I took a bottle with me, a flat bottle, hidden underneath my things, and, a few hours after giving birth, I had a swig of it.

"A drunkard and a whore, that's what I am!"

She raised the bottle to her lips once more and

Laure, who had stood up, tried to wrest it away from her. Betty struggled, suddenly in a rage, trying to scratch and to hurt her. She had a nasty taste in her mouth and panted between her teeth:

"You, too, you're just like the rest of them and I'll show you . . ."

She didn't finish the sentence, suddenly letting go of the bottle, standing there in the middle of the room, under the lamp, her arms dangling, so amazed that her face was totally expressionless.

Laure had just slapped her, calmly, without anger, but so hard that there was a mark on her cheek.

"And now it's time to go to bed. Get undressed."

The strangest thing was that she obeyed, and started taking her clothes off with the movements and the expression of a sleepwalker. A few minutes later, when she was lying between the sheets, she heard Laure's hoarse voice saying:

"Your body is frozen. I'll get you a hot water bottle."

On her way to her room, Laure had taken the bottle of whisky with her.

5

She slept through a smooth, grayish night, as exhausting as a trek through the desert. She didn't dream. There was nothing, no shadows, no lights, no action, no characters, nothing but the listless, monotonous rhythm of her heart which missed a beat from time to time.

Then she heard a bell ringing, but she was so tired she didn't even ask herself whether it was real or imaginary. The noise vibrated through her skull and she hoped that it would stop, that it was one of those bells which announced the departure of a train or a boat, but it grew ever more aggressive and she finally realized that it was the telephone next to her bed.

She didn't want to talk. It was only in order to stop the din that she lifted the receiver and let it drop onto the pillow.

Then a distant voice, as deformed as though it were coming out of a broken-down old phonograph, said:

"Madame Etamble! . . . Madame Etamble! . . . Are you there? . . . Can you hear me? . . . Madame Etamble! . . . Madame Etamble! . . ."

She finally stammered:

"Who is it?"

"It's the hotel switchboard, Madame Etamble. You gave me quite a fright. The telephone's been ringing for five minutes. I was going to send somebody up."

"Why?"

The night before Laure had given her two sleeping pills but that wasn't why she was aching. A spring must have snapped at a certain moment, when she wasn't paying attention to it, and it was now as though a contact had been broken somewhere inside her.

"There's a call from Paris for you."

She didn't react, didn't think of her husband or of anyone else who might have telephoned her. The room was dark, with just a very pale light between the shutters.

"I'll put you through."

She wanted to go back to sleep.

"Is that you, Betty?"

She didn't recognize the voice. She had already closed her eyes and her breathing was becoming heavier.

"This is Florent speaking."

She mumbled reluctantly:

"Yes."

"Can you hear me?"

"Yes."

"I can't hear you at all well. Are you all right?"

"Yes."

He was in a world of light, he was up, washed, shaven, dressed, in the midst of life.

"I saw Guy early this morning. You gave him quite a fright by not letting him know where you were. It was only last night that he got your address from the driver."

His name was Florent Montaigne. He was a friend of Guy's, a friend of the family. He was sure of himself because he was an excellent lawyer.

"Are you sure everything's all right?"

"Yes."

"You're not ill, are you? You sound very far away. Are you still in bed?"

"Yes."

"Can I talk to you?"

He added, hesitantly:

"Are you alone?"

"Yes."

"Guy told me what happened and told me to get in touch with you. The sooner the better, you know. If it's all right with you, I could come to Versailles this afternoon, preferably in the late afternoon, and we could dine together."

"Not today."

"Tomorrow morning then? I can't make it tomorrow afternoon because I'm appearing in court."

"Not tomorrow."

"When?"

"I don't know. I'll call you."

"Are you sure everything's all right and that you don't need a hand?"

"Positive. Good-by, Florent."

She made the necessary effort to stretch out her arm and hang up. The door of the adjoining room was half open and through it Betty could see that Laure had drawn the curtains, that daylight was streaming in, and that life had begun. It seemed to her that, for the first time for days, the sun was shining.

Laure must have heard. She would obviously come in and ask her if she needed anything and Betty didn't want to see her or to talk to her.

It wasn't because of the slap which she remembered just as she remembered everything she had said the day before.

On the contrary, the slap had done her good and, if she had been able to, she would have slapped herself in order to put an end to her hysteria.

Until then she had spent her time escaping from herself. She knew what that meant. She knew herself well. The slap that she should have received years ago had suddenly cast her into reality.

There was no longer that equivocal quality which she managed to give to what she said and what she thought, no longer any artificial warmth, any imprecision.

Instead she was now faced with the truth in its crudest form, in black and white, spelled out simply and cruelly.

And that was something which she couldn't communicate. It was taxing enough even to think about it. It was dangerous.

She had cheated this time as she had so many other times, instinctively, because it was part of her nature. An innate need to protect herself?

She always managed to make things bearable in the end, to stop them being too ugly, too heartbreaking.

She wouldn't talk to Laure or to anybody else any more. She didn't have the strength. She was inert and empty. She didn't want to do anything, only to lie motionless in bed, her eyes open, staring at a corner of the mirror where she could see a little daylight and one of the flowers on the curtain.

It didn't occur to her to ask Florent for news of her husband or her children. As for him, he didn't seem surprised about what had happened and was only alarmed when he didn't recognize her voice. Admittedly, he had known a very different Betty.

Florent was married and his wife, Odette, a lively, witty woman, attracted Guy.

From time to time, the two couples used to go out

together. Last winter they had been to the theater and, on their way out, had decided to have something to eat in a brasserie on Place Blanche. When they were getting into their cars, Florent had said:

"You're taking my wife? I'll take yours, in that case."

Hardly had he started the car than the lawyer, driving with one hand, started to caress Betty with the other. There had never been anything between them. He had never courted her. He had never said anything. He still didn't say anything and, looking straight ahead, threaded his way through the traffic.

It didn't even occur to him that she would say no and, with a docility which he seemed to expect, she too had put out her hand.

The day before she had told Laure that when she was eleven, unlike some of her other friends at La Pommeraye, she had refused to touch the boys.

It was true. Like everything else she had said. Yet it was only one aspect of the truth, the aspect that can be communicated.

What had held her back just then, in spite of her curiosity, was the fear of dirtying herself, of dirtying herself materially. Only much later did the word "dirty" assume another meaning and become an obsession, possibly because she had heard her mother say it too often.

"Don't touch it, Betty. It's dirty!"

"Don't pick your nose. It's dirty!"

And, if she spilled a glass of milk:

"Just like you! You've made a mess again!"

She was a dirty, messy girl. Her father was dirty, too, her mother used to tell him so often enough.

"You ought to change your coverall, Robert. This one is stiff with dirt."

There were dirty customers and clean customers.

"Madame Rochet is filthy."

Madame Van Horn's house, on the other hand, was so clean that one could eat off the floor.

Betty wanted to be dirty in order to be like her father. She couldn't forgive her mother for badgering him as though she had certain rights over him, while it was he who was the head of the family.

"Are you coming down? You're not going to spend all evening doing your filthy experiments, are you?"

He laughed. He never got angry. But in his workshop where he had set up a laboratory, he may have mimicked his wife just as he mimicked his customers in order to make Betty laugh at table.

She had longed to be older, to be her father's wife, to treat him as he deserved.

She tried to go back to sleep, to stop thinking, but even when she stopped thinking, she had the same feeling of irremediability.

She had put everything off for as long as she could, because of Bernard, the doctor with the hypodermic needles who had picked her up on Rue de Ponthieu and had taken her to The Hole instead of to the nearest hotel as she had expected. And then, because of her meeting with Laure who had tried to rescue her, everything had become confused.

On two or three occasions since then, she had given way to a vague feeling of hope. She had talked her fill, skirting the truth and making sure that she never touched the heart of the matter.

It was true and it was untrue that she had wanted to be dirty out of a sort of mystical protest. She would also have liked to have been clean. All her life she had had a nostalgia for order and for cleanliness, and that was why she had married Guy.

She had been working in an office at the time, on Boulevard Haussmann, two minutes walk from Boulevard Malesherbes and the National Mining Board. They had met in a snackbar where Guy used to have a sandwich when he didn't have time to go home for lunch.

At the beginning, it had never occurred to her that it could be serious. She was embarrassed by the fact that he didn't ask her to go to bed with him as all the other men had done and, in the end, out of sheer decency, she had almost insisted.

When she realized that he loved her, when he talked about marriage, she had been so panic-stricken that she had decided never to see him again.

"I must tell you something, Guy . . ."

"Tell me what? That you don't love me enough?"

"You know that that's not true."

"Then what?"

"I'd rather you didn't marry me. It would be better that way."

"Why, if I may ask?"

"Because of everything. Because of me, because of my life."

She had intended to tell him everything, everything she had done, everything she had almost done.

"Look, Betty. I wasn't born yesterday. What you did in the past has nothing to do with me and has nothing to do with you any more. It's all over, do you see? Do you love me?"

"Yes."

She thought she did. She was sure she did. She probably still loved him. She surely still loved him, since she continued to hurt herself.

"In that case, you must get it into your head that life is beginning now; it's as though we had just met, and on Saturday I shall take you to Lyons and introduce you to my mother."

He thought it was easy. Indeed it *was* easy for him. He never looked back. He had made up his mind about the position she would occupy and he had put her there. So there were no problems.

"I can't even run a house."

"Olga is there for that; she would give notice if I had the misfortune to marry a woman who meddled in the housekeeping."

She ended up by believing him and had entered her new role full of goodwill and enthusiasm.

That was all a mistake. Not only because of her past.

It was all a mistake because she and Guy were never

after the same thing. He used to say, proudly and protectively:

"You're my wife!"

Wasn't that enough? His wife! The mother of his children! The woman he came home to every evening in order to tell her about his worries and his hopes.

"You're looking pale today."

"It's because I haven't been out."

"You shouldn't spend so much time indoors. I'll get Menière to look at you."

Their doctor. If something went wrong, Guy always turned to Menière. And if she had shouted out, as she had often wanted to, "Take some notice of me!" he would have replied in perfectly good faith: "You're the only person I take any notice of!"

Admittedly, he worried about her health, bought her dresses and little presents, and frequently sent her flowers.

"Take some notice of *me*. Don't you understand that word?"

Take some notice of herself, of her innermost self, of the being she really was. Not treat her according to his needs, but according to hers.

It was basically out of cowardice, for his own personal convenience, for his peace of mind, that he had not let her confess. She had tried several times. Every time he had put his finger to his lips and smiled.

"What have we decided?"

It was too easy. He wanted the agreeable, convenient side of her which suited his life, and simply passed over whatever might have complicated their relationship with a gesture that resembled a blessing.

The moment something ceased to exist for him it shouldn't exist for her, either.

"Aren't you happy with me?"

"Yes, I am."

"Why don't you go out with Marcelle more often? She's a bit quiet, but she's a nice girl and improves on closer acquaintance."

Only one person had ever really taken any notice of her: her father.

When she was still a little girl, he, the harum-scarum, had realized that he had the embryo of a woman in front of him and he had treated her as such.

Since she was too young when the war separated them, they could never have any long conversations. Most of the time they were together they either played games or joked, and yet, from a mere look in her father's eyes, from the way he might squeeze her hand, she felt that he understood her and that for him she was a human being.

She now even wondered whether he had known her so well that he was worried about her future.

Later, Schwartz had almost been the second man. She had hoped he would be until she realized that she was just a sort of guinea pig for him. He had known her, too. He had taken her to pieces like a mechanic. He had forced her to face up to things that she had always refused to see. He would interrupt her, laughing:

"Watch out. You're sublimating things again!"

That was his favorite word. Yet, despite his cynicism, he was sometimes moved.

"You'd so much like to be a heroine, my poor Betty! I'm beginning to think that that's your undoing. You set your sights so high, you form such a high idea of what you could be, of what you should be, that you fall a little lower each time.

"You're a liar. You're frittering away your life by lying to yourself, you don't dare to face yourself as you are.

"When you get bored or feel uncomfortable, you start telling yourself lies, instead of going to the movies or buying shoes or dresses, as others do."

On one occasion, overexcited as she often used to be with him, she had talked a great deal and he had muttered, half serious, half joking:

"You'll end up in the morgue or in a psychiatric ward."

Had he harmed her? Had he done her any good? His diagnosis was perfectly correct since she really was on the verge of ending up in the morgue or in a hospital.

She heard some muffled steps. Laure had been too tactful to come in immediately after the telephone call, but, now that she didn't hear anything, she came to make sure that Betty had gone to sleep again.

Betty could have closed her eyes and pretended, but she was too weary to cheat.

"I thought you were asleep."

She didn't move her head, didn't try to smile. She

didn't want to have any contact with anybody that morning, or even to see anybody. She felt she was beyond that. She had tried. She had drunk. She had talked till she could talk no more. She had more or less falsified the truth, for her own benefit more than for anyone else's, and she had found it again when she woke up, in spite of everything.

It wasn't worth starting all over again!

"I hope you didn't get any bad news?"

Out of charity rather than out of politeness, she shook her head.

"Aren't you hungry! Don't you want me to order your breakfast?"

For a second she was tempted by the idea of bacon and eggs, but she knew that if she yielded she would have to start all over again.

Then there would be more whisky, more excitement, the need to talk still more. . . . What was the point since there was no way out?

"Not even a cup of coffee?"

Laure frowned, took hold of her wrist, keeping her eyes on her watch. Her lips moved. Betty examined her as though she were seeing her for the first time, and told herself that she couldn't ever have been pretty. She had a man's features. Only her brown, very gentle, very warm eyes contradicted the masculinity of her appearance.

She followed the figures with her lips: "Forty-nine . . . fifty . . . . fifty- one . . . . fifty-two. . . ."

Laure stopped in surprise.

"Do you often have these sudden drops in your pulse beat?"

What was the point in answering? Answering what?

"Would you rather remain in the dark?"

She at last opened her mouth slightly to murmur:

"I don't mind."

It must have been stuffy in the room and Laure went to draw back the curtains and open the shutters. Instead of the flowers, Betty now saw a little piece of sky and the treetops in the mirror.

"Yet you didn't have a bad night, did you? I didn't hear you move. Do you feel any pain anywhere?"

She shook her head.

"A headache?"

She shook her head a second time. She wanted to get it over with as soon as possible, to be left on her own again.

"Would you mind very much if I called a doctor? I know one here in Versailles. He looks after me and he's very good. I promise he won't ask you any indiscreet questions."

She repeated crossly, as though she were forced to make an unnecessary effort:

"I don't mind."

"Would you like me to give you a sponge bath?"

Her skin must have been shining. She was sweating. She could smell the sweat but she shook her head all the same and Laure, who realized that she was disturbing her, went into her own room and picked up the telephone anxiously.

"Hello, Blanche, give me 537 . . . Yes . . . I'll hold on. . . ."

Betty could hear, although it all seemed to happen in another world that didn't concern her.

"Hello . . . Mademoiselle Francine? . . . Is the doctor at home? . . . May I speak with him? I'm not disturbing him, am I? . . . Hello! . . . . Doctor? This is Laure Lavancher. . . . No, I'm very well . . . I'm not calling you because of me but because of a friend of mine who's staying with me. I'd like you to see her. . . . It's hard to say. . . . Last night I gave her two pills of phenobarbital and this morning her pulse rate is fifty-three. No! I don't think she's allergic to anything. . . . Twenty-eight years old. . . . Thank you, doctor . . . I'll be waiting for you . . . You can come straight up. . . ."

She hesitated to go into Betty's room and she could be heard lighting a cigarette and going toward the window which she opened. She finished her cigarette, breathing in the fresh air, before coming back to the door.

"It's one o'clock. The doctor will be coming around at about a quarter to two, before his office opens. Wouldn't you rather tidy yourself up a little? Are you sure you don't want anything to eat?"

Betty simply blinked.

"I'm going to have a snack sent up for myself. If you need anything, don't hesitate to call me."

She pressed a button and a bell could be heard ringing at the end of the corridor. As she waited, she poured herself a drink. Betty could hardly bear to think of the yellow whisky flowing into the glass.

She had the impression that she could even smell it and she wondered how she could ever have drunk it.

If any man other than Bernard had picked her up at the Ponthieu, she would probably have been in a hospital bed by now, with rows of other invalids, and with nurses and a house doctor making his rounds at regular intervals.

Wasn't that what she had been looking for subconsciously for three days and three nights? She hadn't really thought about it. She had had so few moments of real lucidity that she had hardly thought at all.

All she knew was that she was sinking ever deeper, that she was doing so in an almost frenzied manner, and that it was a relief.

It was an act of defiance, a means of revenge. It was also an end. She had dirtied herself to the core, as much as she could, without any possible means of return.

That was bound to happen. It had been brewing in her for months and she had been defying destiny deliberately in order to bring about the catastrophe.

Of course, there had also been the affair with Schwartz in the past, and the incident with Florent in the car which hadn't led anywhere because Florent was too cautious.

There had been other episodes, too, and, in the afternoon, she had occasionally gone to certain discreet bars not far from where she lived, on Rue de l'Etoile or Rue Brey, for instance, which were full of couples sitting in the twilight and men waiting and chatting with the barman.

It was in one of these bars that she had met Philippe, an ungainly secretive boy who played the saxophone in a nightclub on Rue Marbeuf. Philippe didn't ask her questions, as Schwartz had done. He spoke very little and usually just looked at her pensively.

"What are you thinking about?" she asked.

"You."

"What do you think of me?"

He replied with a vague gesture.

"It's very complicated."

When she lay in bed after making love, he took hold of his saxophone and improvised tunes that were both ironic and tender. She didn't know anything about him except that his mother was Russian and that he had a sister. He lived in a furnished apartment on Rue de Montenotte where Betty had even darned his socks as a joke.

He knew she was married and had children because she had told him, but he never asked her any questions.

In the end, he became a necessity. The hours spent in the apartment on Avenue de Wagram were a time of gray indifference, like time wasted in a waiting room. She always longed for the afternoon when she could join Philippe. The concierge greeted her as she passed and called her "the pretty little lady." It was Betty who arrived with bottles bought at the grocer's on Place des Ternes, with sweets and tidbits.

He wasn't quite twenty-four and had remained awkward, defenseless in life, indifferent to his future. When she tried to inspire him with ambition, he simply smiled a slightly veiled smile.

"You're talking like my sister."

It was as though he were unaware of the fact that millions of people lived all around him, jostled each other, elbowed each other out of the way; even in their midst, on the street, he carried with him a sort of halo of solitude.

"What would you do if I didn't come to see you?"

"I don't know, since you do come. Maybe I'd go and get you."

"Where?"

"At your house."

"What about my husband?"

He didn't answer. He didn't ask himself any questions, either.

"Tomorrow?"

"Tomorrow."

But the next day Betty had not been able to go to Rue de Montenotte. General Etamble's widow had arrived in Paris unannounced, when a friend of hers who had a chauffeur offered her a lift at the last minute. Marcelle had an appointment with the dentist which she couldn't put off and it was Betty who had to keep her mother-in-law company.

It was Elda's day off. She had gone to see a friend in the suburbs and would only take the last train back, just before midnight.

After lunch, when he was about to leave for the office, Guy had told his wife:

"I'll leave Mother in your hands for the afternoon and I'll take her to the theater tonight."

For she had come to Paris mainly to see a new play. The afternoon had been endless, and Betty hadn't had a single moment in which to call Philippe before Marcelle came back from the dentist.

"I can't speak now. There are people next door. I can't get away this afternoon, but I'll call you this evening at about nine."

When Elda was away, it was the maid who looked after the children, but since Madame Etamble was there, Betty had to act as the real mother.

They had dined early at Antoine's. Guy and his mother had left for the theater. When Betty returned to the third floor, Olga was still lingering in the apartment.

"You can go to bed. I'm not going to budge."

Perhaps Olga suspected something, because she seemed reluctant to go up to her room on the seventh floor.

"Hello! Is that you?"

He replied ironically with a few bars on the saxophone.

"Are you unhappy?"

He played a comical glissando.

"Answer me, Philippe. I'm at the end of my tether. If only you knew what an afternoon I've had."

"And how about me?"

"Did you miss me? Listen. You know where I live. The children are asleep. It's the nurse's day off. The maid has just gone to bed and my husband is at the theater."

"So?"

"Don't you see?"

"Yes."

"You don't seem to be enthusiastic about it."

He hesitated.

"I've wanted to do this for such a long time. You'll understand better when you're here."

She had waited behind the door in her dressing gown, wondering why he took such a long time. When he was with her at last, she felt she had almost lost him and she clung to him, her lips pressed against his.

"This way."

She took him to the drawing room and made a sign to him to walk on tiptoe and to talk in a whisper.

"Are you frightened?"

"No."

"Aren't you pleased to see where I live?"

She pointed to the piano, the velvet wallpaper, the gilded frames.

"Come closer."

She was feverish, with a strange gleam in her eyes. She wanted to see him on the family sofa where she had spent so many evenings sitting next to Marcelle and where the general's widow had sat that afternoon.

It was her revenge. She had had to insist that Philippe come, and if he hadn't come she would have been deeply disappointed. The word "dirty" didn't enter her mind at the time, but that was just what she wanted to do to the room, to the apartment, to everything.

"You look unhappy. Are you nervous?"

She jumped up, pulled off her dressing gown, and pretended to dance, naked, in the middle of the Etambles' drawing room.

"How about the children?" he objected.

"They're there, behind that door. There's a passage and another door on the left that leads to their room. They're asleep. Wait a minute!"

She opened the door ajar.

"So if Marcelle gets up, we'll hear her."

He didn't share her excitement and stood there awkwardly as though he realized that any man here, that evening, would have put her in the same frantic state.

She was suddenly paying off an old score, not so much with her husband as with the family, a whole world, a way of life, a way of thinking.

She took the initiative with exaggerated boldness, forced him to take her, and he saw her eyes sparkling with triumph, her small teeth clenched close to his face.

"Come to Mummy. I'll phone Antoine to come down. Lie down on the . . ."

Neither Betty nor Philippe had heard the door of the apartment opening or the sound of footsteps upon the hall rug. The windowed door of the drawing room opened in its turn and the lovers remained for a moment immobile, too startled to think of separating.

Philippe, who hadn't undressed, was on his feet first and stood, head bowed, awaiting whatever the husband might do.

As for Guy, he stood with frozen face, supporting his mother who had felt unwell at the theater; then he gestured to the man to leave.

Betty, still naked, was obliged to retrieve her wrapper from the center of the room, while her mother-in-law, being helped to the sofa, cried out:

"Not on this."

Her son eased her into an armchair.

"Quickly! Give me my drops! In my bag! Twenty drops. . . ."

He ran to the kitchen, returned with a glass of water, and almost collided with Betty in the corridor as she was going to their room.

She knew that it was all over and she didn't care. All she hoped now was that everything should happen as quickly as possible, and she dressed with jerky, abrupt movements, putting on a dark suit and a black hat.

She hoped to be able to leave by the back stairs, to avoid a confrontation. Somebody must have anticipated that because Marcelle knocked at the door.

"Guy asks you to come to the drawing room."

Antoine was there, too. Madame Etamble's chest was heaving tempestuously.

Guy had become a stranger, as cold and methodical

as one might imagine an important banker to be. He was talking on the telephone in his study, the door open.

"Thank you, Maître Aubernois. That's all right, then. As long as you've understood what I want. . ."

He stood up, turned toward his wife without curiosity, without any apparent anger, indeed, without any sort of emotion.

"Come here."

"Where?"

"Here. Sit down. Write."

" . . . *give up all my maternal rights and undertake to sign all future documents that* . . ."

It wasn't happening on earth, in a large city, in a house where people were sleeping peacefully, but in a nightmare world where every gesture was in slow motion and went on forever, where toneless voices sounded like echoes.

"Here's a check to tide you over. As soon as you let me know your address, I'll send you your belongings. My lawyer will get in touch with you."

Even Madame Etamble had risen to her feet as people do in church or at moments of great solemnity. Her hands were clasped over her chest. Her lips were quivering as though she was about to say something, but she didn't utter a word.

All four of them, standing very stiffly, watched Betty walk past them to the door.

She hadn't asked to kiss her children for the last time. She hadn't said anything. She forgot to close the door and one of the four, she didn't know who, had broken away from the tableau and closed the door behind her.

She didn't take the elevator, and once she was on the sidewalk, she started walking very quickly through the rain, hugging the walls.

BETTY

6

"Come in, doctor."

Dressed in navy blue, his black bag in his hand, he looked like one of those Frenchmen marching behind a flag down the Champs Elysees, and he wore a boutonnière of multicolored ribbons in his lapel. He obviously believed that life was to be taken seriously and, in the presence of a patient, he behaved with earnest deliberation.

"So you're feeling ill," he said, as one might tune an instrument, standing in the middle of the room and looking Betty up and down, though she didn't even bat her eyelashes in order to greet him. "We'll soon see about that. Do you mind if I wash my hands?"

He knew the way to the bathroom. He must have known every room in the hotel. He came back rubbing his palms gently, and drew up a chair by her bedside.

"Are you feeling very bad?" he asked, taking Betty's wrist and feeling her pulse.

She shook her head.

"No pain anywhere? No headache? No contractions in your chest or in your stomach?"

She continued to answer by gestures and he turned toward Laure who was slipping out of the door.

"Please stay. Unless your friend has anything against it. Her pulse is sixty now."

He didn't seem at all surprised by his patient's behavior; it was as though he came across identical cases every day. Putting his bag on the bed, he took out a sphygmometer with which he seemed to have difficulty.

"Hold out your left arm . . . not too stiff . . . Fine . . . I'm simply testing your blood pressure. . . ."

She saw him staring at the little needle on the dial with a serious expression while she felt her blood throbbing in her arteries. He did it twice, three times.

"Do you usually have low blood pressure?"

And, turning to Laure, as though he no longer expected Betty to give him any information:

"What did she have this morning? Has she had breakfast?

"She didn't want anything."

"Not even a cup of coffee?"

"No."

One could almost feel him thinking, following a line of reasoning to which he was as accustomed as a circus horse that automatically changes step at the same point in the ring. With the same precise, meticulous gestures he put the sphygmometer back in his case and produced a stethoscope which he put to his ears.

"Breathe through your mouth. . . Good . . . Again . . . Go on . . . Now cough. . . ."

She did as he said, noticing that he had tufts of hair in his nose and in his ears.

"Breathe in again . . . Gently . . . That's enough . . . Can you sit up?"

She pulled herself up with more difficulty than she would have thought, wearily, listlessly.

"It won't take long. . . ."

He applied the metal disk to two or three points on her back, and came back to one point, the highest, as though he had discovered something abnormal.

"Hold your breath . . . Good . . . Breathe in . . . You can lie down again. . . ."

Putting the instrument to her chest, he concentrated on a point that must have corresponded to the one he had tested on her back. When he listened to her breathing, his eyes became fixed and expressionless, like the eyes of a fowl.

"Does a doctor see you regularly?"

"Not really."

She had spoken without realizing it, reluctantly, for she had wanted to submit herself to this examination without taking any part in it.

"Have you had any serious illnesses?"

"Scarlet fever, when I was three."

The stethoscope was now hanging around his neck and, with his bare hand, he felt the upper part of her torso, pressing his fingers between her ribs.

"Does this hurts?"

"No."

"And here?"

"Slightly."

"And here?"

"A bit more."

"Do you often feel pain just here?"

"Not in any particular place. All over my chest."

Pulling back the sheets, he felt her stomach through her nightgown.

"Have you had a bowel movement this morning?"

"No."

"How about yesterday?"

"I can't remember. No. I didn't yesterday either."

With the same serious expression, he produced another instrument, a little nickel hammer.

"Don't be frightened."

She knew what he was going to do. It wasn't the first time that she had been examined like this. Then he scratched the soles of her feet with a pointed object, a metal toothpick which he had taken out of his waistcoat pocket and which reminded her of Bernard and his rabbits.

"Can you feel anything?"

"Yes."

"Now?"

"Yes."

He glanced at Laure whom he obviously regarded as if she were the mother, or elder sister, or a nurse. His last gesture before putting away his instruments had been to raise her eyelids.

"Do you ever have fits of dizziness?"

"I've had some in the last few days."

"Strong enough to lose your balance?"

"No."

"Have you had an emotional shock?"

She didn't answer. It was Laure who nodded.

"Besides," said Laure, "we both had a great deal to drink. Last night I gave her two phenobarbital tablets of ten centigrams. She slept quite calmly. She was awakened by the telephone and she's been like that ever since."

He turned toward Betty and tapped her on the forearm.

"To begin with, you must realize that there is nothing organically wrong with you and that you'll be perfectly all right after a good rest."

He seemed to be asking Laure for advice before going on.

"My friend is alone here, doctor. She's going through a difficult period."

"I understand! I understand! Of course, the best thing would be a period in a nursing home. Have you anything against that?"

Without looking at him, Betty said:

"I don't want to go to a nursing home."

"Mind you, I'm not insisting. If you have the courage to look after yourself, and above all to discipline yourself, you'll recover as well here as you will anywhere else. Do you have many visitors?"

"None," Laure answered for her.

"Just as well. Don't go out either, not for four or five days at least, and then only for short walks in the garden of the hotel. Nothing to eat until tomorrow morning except for a light vegetable soup tonight."

He had produced a notebook from his pocket and was conscientiously writing down everything he said. No visits. Stay indoors for five days. Liquid diet until . . . He paused for a moment to remember the day of the week . . . until Saturday morning. . . .

"You're not afraid of injections, are you?"

She was being treated like a child or like an idiot.

"I'll give you an injection before I go, and tonight you must take one of the pills I'm going to prescribe for you. Take one every night for three days. And, twice a day, at lunchtime and dinnertime, a small dose of reserpine!"

He took a sterilized hypodermic syringe out of a metal box surrounded by adhesive strips, broke off the tip of an ampule, and his movements, his voice, were like a ritual, a religious ceremony.

"Turn over slightly . . . that's enough. . . ."

He took hold of her nightgown with two fingers and pulled it up without uncovering her groin. "That didn't hurt too much, did it?"

It was all over. He put his instruments back into his bag.

"Madame Lavancher will call me if you need me before tomorrow evening. Otherwise, I'll drop by when my office closes, between six and seven."

He looked around for his hat which he had left in Laure's room and suddenly, while he was talking to Laure in the corridor, Betty was sorry she had let him go.

He had only made some professional gestures, said things which she knew so well that she could tell exactly what he was going to say next and yet, for a short time, he had put her back into a reassuring, familiar world.

For a quarter of an hour, somebody had paid attention to her, as though she were worth it, as though her life were important.

What was he saying to Laure? The wife of a doctor, she had been able to follow on his face all the hypotheses that he eliminated one after the other. Was she telling him what had happened to Betty, or at least what she knew?

For she didn't know everything. She didn't know the worst part. Besides, Laure had belonged to *their* milieu, in spite of everything. Whatever she did, she, like the doctor, remained partially on their side.

There wouldn't have been any point in talking to them, because they wouldn't have understood.

"Do you want to get some rest?"

She blinked again.

"You have absolutely no cause for anxiety. I had a word with the doctor in the corridor. At one point when he was examining you, I saw that he was worried. He obviously thought he had spotted some neuro-circulatory trouble—nothing particularly serious, but it can be a bore.

"But now he's quite sure. You're simply suffering from the aftereffect of what you've been through in the last few days. I'll be looking after you and I warn you that I'm going to be very strict."

Her good humor was to no avail. Betty didn't react.

"You'll probably doze for two or three hours. That'll be the effect of the injection. I'll order vegetable soup for you and I'll leave you for the time being. See you later, Betty."

Maybe she was wrong in refusing to go to a nursing home. She would have been sent to one of those places on the outskirts of Paris about which one periodically reads in the papers that such and such a film star is having a health cure. That seemed a dreary idea to her. It was dreary here, too, but at least there was the possibility of leaving without asking anyone's permission. And, when she was less weary, she would leave.

She heard the telephone ringing next door, and Laure's muffled voice.

"Yes . . . Yes . . . No . . . She's all right . . .

She's in bed, yes . . . The doctor's been . . . I'll tell you all about it . . . Not immediately . . . What? . . . Let's say two . . . That's right . . . I'll see you later. . . ."

She was sure that it was Mario. Mario who wanted to come within an hour and Laure telling him to wait a couple of hours to be sure that Betty was asleep.

But she knew she wouldn't sleep. The injection had made her body numb, it had made her lids, her hot lids, heavy, but it didn't send her to sleep.

She continued to think, above all in images, and all the images were of the same monotonous gray, with less contrasts than in the morning and less dramatic substance.

She went through them wearily, as she might turn over the pages of a book she was obliged to peruse. It seemed important to her, a duty she had to perform.

The words may not have had their customary meaning in her mind but, as far as she was concerned, they were clear and that was the main thing.

She had to face up to things instead of always trying to run away. And drinking in order to obtain the illusion of courage and then to talk to Laure feverishly and finally to collapse was not the same as facing up to things.

She had always felt that there would be a catastrophe in the end, even before she met Guy. As a child, she had looked at the other little girls as though they possessed something which she didn't have, even though there were times when she was pleased, not to say proud, to be herself, because it seemed to her that it was she who was most complete.

Now that problem was over. The catastrophe had taken place. She hadn't said anything to them as she went toward the door, as they stood there, all four of them, watching her leave. Had she felt ashamed? After the event, she very much wanted to persuade herself that she hadn't felt ashamed, because if she had, that would have meant that they were right and she was wrong.

She could no longer remember whether she had lowered her head or whether she had looked them in the eyes. She must have looked at them since she could still see the expression on each of their faces.

Why had she signed without protesting? Out of pride? Out of indifference?

Yet, once she was outside, in the rain, she had started running close to the houses and she had arrived breathless, as if she were searching for a refuge, in the bar that was lit up at the corner of Avenue de Wagram and Place des Ternes.

There had been a great many people, a red copper counter, trays full of glasses of beer being carried past on a level with her head, and, seated at the tables, men and women eating.

"A whisky."

"With ice?"

"Yes. Make it a double."

"Soda water?"

"I don't care."

She almost tore it out of the barman's hands and drank it avidly, while some of the people standing around her looked at her disapprovingly.

"Bring another."

She fumbled for money in her bag and the check almost fell onto the sawdust. She caught it in mid-air. Would she have bent down to pick it up from the floor? Perhaps not.

She had a drink and then resumed her walk, as fast as before, the raindrops on her face. She made her way between the cars to Rue de Montenotte and, her heart beating, rushed toward the elevator.

The concierge opened the glass door of his office.

"He's not there, Madame."

"Hasn't he come back yet?"

"He came back about half an hour ago, but he came down ten minutes later with his suitcase and his instrument. He asked me to call him a cab. He seemed in such a hurry that I thought he had a train to catch.

"'Is your sister ill?' I asked him.

"Because I know from the letters she writes to him that she lives in Rouen."

"What did he say?"

"He didn't say anything. He looked frightened. When I asked whether he was going to be gone a long time, he shrugged his shoulders.

"'You can do what you like with the apartment.'

"That's that! I suppose he's not going to come back.

Since he'd payed the rent in advance, I couldn't stop him, especially since the taxi arrived almost immediately and he gave me a good tip."

She had no idea what the time was just then, and from then on, for three days and three nights, she was going to lose all sense of time, of meals and sleep.

She had cried as she walked along the dark sidewalks, without noticing what direction she was going in, and she had even talked to herself.

She had found herself back on Avenue MacMahon, and, still taking the darkest streets, she had reached Porte Maillot.

She had gone into a bar, the smallest and darkest bar. She had ordered a whisky. There wasn't any, so she drank brandy and water while a heavily made-up woman with a large behind, perched insecurely on her stiletto heels, watched her, trying to understand.

She must have been getting drunk by then, but she wasn't aware of it and her one idea was still to find Philippe. She had gone in the wrong direction. She would have to go back the same way. It didn't even occur to her to take a taxi and besides, Philippe didn't start work before midnight.

It couldn't have been that late yet. He must have had to put his suitcase somewhere before going to his nightclub. He had been frightened by Guy, that was perfectly natural.

She wanted to reassure him. She was now free. She wouldn't impose herself on him. He was too young to take on a woman. Still, he could see as much of her as he liked.

She walked on, trying not to lose sight of the Arc de Triomphe. She didn't know how much money she had in her handbag. If Philippe needed any money, there was the check which she was ready to give him.

She had had to stop. A man had seized her by the arm, had said something obscene to her, and she had been panic-stricken.

The nightclub where Philippe worked was called The Taxi. She had never been there. She couldn't find it. She looked at one neon sign after the other and it was the doorman of another nightclub who had pointed to the least luminous sign, in little dark red letters, at the far end of the street.

It was stifling inside. The club was smaller than the drawing room in the apartment on Avenue de Wagram, full of smoke and shrill music. Groups of men were leaning against the bar and, a yard away from them, a woman was undressing beneath a spotlight.

The members of the orchestra were wearing pale-blue dinner jackets. She looked for Philippe, but couldn't see him.

"Isn't Philippe here?" she asked the barman, standing on the tip of her toes.

"Which Philippe? The saxophonist?"

"Yes."

"I don't know. I can't see him. He must have got somebody to sit in for him."

A man wanted to offer her a drink and had already put his hand on her thighs.

Not yet. Not here. Philippe had left his rooms and hadn't come to work. That meant that he had done the same thing as Schwartz.

Disappeared. Vanished into thin air in Paris. If she wanted to find him, she would have had to spend every day going from one nightclub to the other, from Place de l'Etoile to Montmartre and Montparnasse. She would have had to explore every single place where music was played.

"As soon as you let me know your address," her husband had said.

The logical solution was to go to a hotel and take a room before having her things sent. But how could she stay on her own, between four walls, slip into a bed and go to sleep?

Another bar. She hadn't had anything to drink at The Taxi. She needed to get drunk as quickly as possible. She remembered different forms of lighting, nearly always a mirror behind the glasses and the bottles, girls sitting next to her and looking at her with a puzzled expression.

"A whisky . . . Double."

The word "dirty" had come to her mind because of her shoes spattered with mud and her wet feet.

She started to be dirty. She was vaguely aware of wanting to go right to the bottom. Since she had never managed to be the cleanest, wasn't it better to be the dirtiest, while she was at it?

She didn't want to sleep. What she wanted was not to be alone.

She wasn't alone anymore. A man had paid for her drinks, had taken her by the arm, and had pushed her out onto the sidewalk and into a quiet street where one could see the lights of a hotel. They went past a glass door. A red-headed woman, sitting at the reception desk, watched them go by and, raising her head, shouted upstairs:

"Is Room 3 ready, Maria?"

"Immediately, Madame. You can come up."

A narrow corridor with a worn carpet. A strange smell. A door open to a room where the bed was made up, but where a maid was rapidly changing the towels.

"That's a thousand francs, service not included."

Betty was so drunk that once the woman had left she collapsed, fully dressed, onto the bed and almost went to sleep. She could hardly remember the man's face. He was quite fat, with blue eyes, and he wore a large red-gold wedding ring on his finger.

"Take your clothes off!"

She had tried, couldn't manage it, and had dozed off again. He hadn't stayed long. With a look of slight embarrassment, he had put a banknote on Betty's bag.

She was asleep at last, she had plunged into sleep like an elevator with a broken cable.

Somebody shook her by the shoulders.

"Up you get, young woman."

She couldn't understand what they wanted, why she was being treated so roughly.

"Come on! Don't play dumb. The half-hour's up."

"I want to sleep."

"You can sleep somewhere else. If you don't get out, I'll call Monsieur Charles."

He had come down in his shirt sleeves and slippers.

"What's this? You won't leave?"

He pulled her to her feet; she was swaying, her field of vision blurred.

"I can see what's wrong with you. I don't like that sort of thing. Especially since I bet you're not the regular type. I don't want any trouble and I need the room."

She reeled into the street. There were great holes in her memory. She had had some hard-boiled eggs with a cup of coffee that had tasted foul and she had vomited in a dirty lavatory.

A man almost as drunk as she was, with a foreign accent. She no longer knew whether it was that night or the next.

If it was the following night, she had no notion how the previous night had ended.

They had been drinking in a place where all the customers were crushed together; in front of everybody else, he had passed his hand over her behind and her breasts with a satisfied and proprietorial air. Somebody had made some remark and a fight had almost broken out.

It was still raining outside and they had walked arm in arm. She spoke to him about Philippe, trying to explain that there had been a misunderstanding, that he had had no reason to be alarmed, that he was very young and, above all, very gentle.

"He's just a poor kid, understand? I've just got to find him. It's terribly important because he won't dare show up again. He thinks that Guy is furious with him. Guy didn't even look at him; he wouldn't be able to recognize him in the street. The truth, if you want the whole truth, is that Guy knew everything already. You see? He's no fool, Guy!"

She was drunk. Yet she wasn't sure she was wrong. She had thought of it before then. Guy had stopped asking her how she spent her afternoons at a fairly early stage.

Maybe he preferred it that way? Who knows what would have happened if his mother hadn't been with him when he found her with Philippe on the drawing-room sofa?

There was no longer any point in wondering. He had never attached any importance to her past. He loved her in his own fashion, without any complications, with a cozy love. He didn't try to find out what was going on in her head. At the most he might ask her, like a man who knows the answer:

"Is everything all right? Are you happy?"

When she said yes, he didn't ask her anything else.

She could still see herself with the foreigner, in the middle of a street, with cars passing on either side, drivers shouting insults at them, and the man who suddenly asked suspiciously:

"Where are you taking me?"

"I don't know. It's you who're taking me."

"Me! Where would I be taking you?"

They had had a confused argument.

"Don't you know where we can go?"

"No."

"You're not a thief, are you?"

He looked into her eyes as though he wanted to hypnotize her.

"Well, we'll try my hotel. I'm not sure whether they'll let you in."

They had taken a taxi and had got out somewhere near a bar to have a last drink. The hotel was near the Galéries Lafayette, with a marble staircase and a red carpet.

The man had drunk too much to manage anything. Nevertheless, he went on trying, asking Betty to help him. Aching all over, feeling terribly dizzy, she dozed off every five minutes or so and in the end he fell asleep, too.

She could have slept all the next day and perhaps even all the next night. She felt ill. It seemed to her that it was dawn when he made her get dressed because he had an airplane to catch.

It was later than she thought. The sidewalks were black with people with a sea of umbrellas over their heads.

She wandered through the crowd of flesh and blood, an insubstantial being, and from time to time she stopped dead at the edge of the sidewalk to watch the cars go by. She no longer thought about Philippe or

Guy, but occasionally thought about the letter, about the shame of having signed a document by which she sold her two daughters.

That was becoming an obsession, and she talked about it under her breath as she opened the door of a bar.

•

"Come in. Don't make any noise. I think she's asleep."

Mario had knocked so discreetly that Betty hadn't heard anything. But she could hear Laure whispering. She knew that they were kissing each other.

"I'll make sure."

She closed her eyes. She felt someone standing near her bed, leaning over her, moving away making sure that the floorboards didn't creak and leaving the door ajar.

She could no longer distinguish the words, only a murmur as one might hear in a confessional. She heard a bottle being uncorked, glasses being filled. The tone of the conversation was serene, calm, with Mario giving an occasional stifled laugh.

He didn't sit down, but walked to and fro, then the bed creaked slightly as if Laure were lying down on it.

It was getting dark outside. Laure must have been talking about Betty and it seemed to her that at one point Mario had come up to the door and looked through the chink.

In thousands of other rooms, couples must have

been chatting in the twilight at the same time, in the same way, smoking a cigarette and having a drink.

Why had that become so extraordinary for Betty as she lay in bed? Mario always came to see Laure in her room; he was her lover; they saw each other every evening at The Hole where Laure always had dinner.

They spoke to each other softly, simply, calmly, she lying on the bed, he seated in an armchair, and if they wanted to make love, nothing was stopping them. They wouldn't necessarily do it. It wasn't indispensable.

They were happy, trustful, carefree.

An insidious desire developed in Betty. Fate was unfair. She didn't try to specify the nature of this unfairness, but she felt frustrated, as though something of hers had been stolen, as though it was Laure who had stolen something belonging to her.

After all, it was Laure who had chosen her, of all the crazies at The Hole. Hardly had the doctor, obsessed by his little animals, disappeared than she had sat down at her table, a glass in her hand.

Betty hadn't invited her; she hadn't even known about her existence.

Didn't she, the wife of a doctor, realize that Betty had no right to drink, that she had drunk too much already, that she was physically and morally at the end of her tether?

What had she done? She had filled her glass, at least twice, if not more. She had taken her back to the hotel without asking her consent.

She had looked after her, admittedly, but she had given her still more to drink the next day, in order to draw her out, in order to get her to confide in her, in order to add another story to her collection.

Betty lay inertly in the twilight, without any strength or vitality, knocked out by some drug which the doctor had injected into her, and in the meantime they were both chatting next door like two people who understood each other perfectly.

How had Laure deserved to be happy? For she had been happy before, too, for twenty-eight years with her husband, and she had boasted about it. She hadn't been on her own for very long—a year, she said—and she had found Mario almost immediately.

Why she, while Betty had tried so frequently? Nothing worried Laure. She came and went in life, serenely, looking at other people indulgently.

She looked at Betty indulgently, too, and it was precisely indulgence, that sort of indulgence, which she didn't want. What she wanted was what she was entitled to by all her efforts.

There was no justice, no fairness. In a few days' time, or in a few hours' time, room 53 would be empty, Betty would be somewhere else, it little mattered where. And, in the next room, Laure and Mario would continue to see each other every evening.

"What else did she say?"

"She told me so many things that I can't remember. You see, she's unhappy by nature. She'll spend her life chasing after something without ever knowing what."

"She looks lost."

"Maybe she'll end up by finding some good soul who'll adopt her, like a stray dog."

Those weren't necessarily their exact words, but she didn't have the impression that she was making the whole thing up. She was sure that it was basically true and that that was what would happen. Laure would look at Mario contentedly, with relief, because once Betty had left he would no longer feel so sorry for her.

They had stopped talking, and Betty soon understood why.

Would she still be able to make love, after what she had been through for three days and three nights?

There they were, body to body, their saliva in each other's mouths, coming silently, motionlessly, while Betty lay staring at the gray sky and the black trees in the mirror, her nails pressed into her skin. She wanted to shout, to make them stop, to stop them being happy.

She was tempted to get dressed and to leave so that they would find her room empty and feel ashamed of themselves.

She didn't have the strength. Besides, as soon as she appeared in the lobby the porter would probably tell Laure. Hadn't she given him special instructions? The doctor had spoken to her in the corridor and had delegated his authority to her.

He had allowed Betty not to go to a nursing home provided she didn't leave her room, didn't get excited, and didn't receive any visitors.

The chink of the door lit up. They had switched the bedside lamp on next door and Mario said:

"Do you think she's still asleep?"

"If you're worried, go and see," answered Laure, without moving from the bed. "Give me a light first."

"It's strange."

"What?"

"That she should spend so much time asleep."

Betty heard his steps come nearer, then move away again, until he finally came up to the door and pushed it open a little wider.

He moved silently, as one might enter a child's room at night, and tried to distinguish Betty's face in the half-light. In order to get a better view of it, he came a step closer, leaned over, and saw her open eyes and the finger she pressed against her lips.

She smiled at him in complicity, as though she were putting her trust in him, and he smiled back, blinked his eyes as a sign of agreement, went back as silently as he had come and left the door ajar again.

"Well? Is she asleep?"

"It looks like it."

He wasn't really lying, he was just cheating.

"What did I tell you? Give me another drink, will you?"

Betty had closed her eyes at last and breathed calmly.

7

Laure didn't mention Mario's visit to her. Of course she didn't owe Betty any explanations. But the fact was nevertheless significant, and Betty was quite pleased to have something, however small, to hold against her.

She didn't like people who always seemed too perfect. She didn't trust them. After making such a fuss over her, Laure already felt a little weary and wanted to resume her own life, expecially since Betty was in bed and the doctor had said that she couldn't go out or have anything to drink.

"Did you sleep well?"

She cheated, too, when she said yes.

"Are you hungry?"

"I don't know."

"I'll have your vegetable soup sent up. What would you rather? A lot of light or just a little?"

She didn't care. She lay there inertly and that gave her a secret pleasure. Laure switched on the lights, went from one room to the other. The waiter came in with the soup and Betty sat up in bed.

It seemed to both of them that it all took a very long time. Time dragged, that evening, as though each of the two women had something in the back of her mind.

Laure changed in her own room and walked round in circles. Her voice had altered slightly, as though she was overdoing it.

"Wasn't it rather tasteless? Let me put your pillow down. Wouldn't you rather the maid came to make the bed? Don't you want to have a wash?"

All these words, all these sentences, simply in order to say:

"Would you mind very much if I left you for a couple of hours and dined out? It may not be very charitable to talk like that when you're obliged to stay in bed, but I need some air and some exercise. If you need anything, just ring the bell. I'll give instructions to Louisette. If needs be, she'll call me and I'll be back in a few minutes. You're not angry, are you? You don't think I'm abandoning you, do you?"

On the contrary, Betty was delighted that she was going out. She waited impatiently until she was alone and, after about ten minutes, when she was sure that her friend hadn't forgotten something and wasn't going to come back, she got up, closed the door to the adjoining room, for no precise reason, perhaps just symbolically, and went to the bathroom. She didn't feel very strong and she took a long time over her grooming, doing her hair and making herself up discreetly.

As she was selecting a nightgown in a drawer, she found a traveling alarm clock and started to wind it.

"Hello! Can you tell me the time, please."

"Are you feeling better? It's half-past eight. Eight thirty-two, to be precise. Do you need anything?"

"No, thanks."

She set the hands. For the first time since she had left Avenue de Wagram, she was worried about the time, was aware of time, and that was already a return to life.

She would have been capable of getting dressed and going out in spite of the doctor, of calling a taxi and driving to The Hole.

As she looked at herself in the mirror, she was tempted to do so, and she tried to imagine how Laure and Mario would react when they saw her coming in.

She mustn't do that. It wouldn't be any use; quite the contrary. She switched off all the lights except for her bedside lamp and slipped under the sheets.

She had no intention of going to sleep. Nor did she want to go on turning over her depressing memories in her mind. Something was brewing, something which was still very vague, which it wouldn't have been wise to specify, a possible way out.

Yesterday, this morning, even this afternoon, she was convinced that there was no way out. This evening, however, she was waiting for something, she was struggling against the desire to sleep that benumbed her body in spite of all her efforts to resist it, and suddenly, at ten to nine, her hand groped for the bell marked "Waiter."

She needed some coffee. A few minutes more and she would have dropped off to sleep. Jules knocked at the door and murmured anxiously:

"I'll call the maid immediately."

"I don't want the maid."

"Madame Lavancher told me . . . "

"It doesn't matter what she told you. I want a cup of black coffee."

"Ah, that's different."

He hesitated all the same.

"I suppose it's all right for me to get you one. Are you sure it won't harm you?"

A little later he brought her a coffeepot and she sat up in bed. She was waiting for the coffee to filter through when the telephone rang. She stretched out her arm, surprised that she could do it so quickly. A man's voice said:

"Madame Etamble? Did I wake you up? I'm sorry to bother you. There's a Monsieur Etamble who wants to speak to you."

"Did he give his first name?"

She thought it might be Antoine.

"No. I'll ask him."

"Don't bother. Put him through."

"But he's here in the lobby."

In a whisper, as though he were afraid of being overheard by someone standing near him, he added:

"He asked me a great many questions and insisted on knowing whether you were alone or whether you'd had any visitors. . . ."

Not for a second had it occurred to her that Guy might have wanted to see her or even that he should have sent his brother, if it was Antoine who was downstairs. Hadn't Florent, his lawyer, already been in touch with her?

"Send him up."

She had a sip of coffee and then slid down into the bed to resume the position she had been in that afternoon.

Jules, with a surly expression, led the visitor along the corridor, and opened the door for him. It was Guy, hat in hand, diffident, and trying to get used to the dim lighting.

"Am I disturbing you?"

She pointed to a chair with a weary hand, the chair the doctor had sat on by her bedside.

"Sit down."

"When he spoke to you on the telephone, Florent had the impression there was something wrong. He said he hardly recognized your voice. I was afraid you might be ill or that something had happened to you."

"I'm simply very, very tired. I'll get over it."

He looked at her out of the corner of his eye. He was the same as usual, a little more concerned than usual, perhaps, a little awkward. He chose banal sentences on purpose, out of shyness.

"Have you seen a doctor?"

"This afternoon."

"What did he say?"

"That I'd be up in four or five days' time."

"Have you got somebody to look after you?"

She looked automatically at the door of the adjoining room.

"A friend. She's gone out to dinner but she'll be back soon."

She didn't feel any emotion at seeing him and she was quite surprised to establish how alien he seemed to her.

She had difficulty in believing that she was his wife, that she had lived with him for six years, sleeping every night in his bed, that they had had two children together, made of a part of each of them.

Did Guy have the same impression? He too looked at her furtively as though he were trying to think of what to say next.

It was she who spoke. "Are the children all right?"

"Fine, except that Charlotte has a cold and is cross about having to stay at home."

"Has your mother gone back to Lyons?"

"Not yet. She's staying with Antoine. She's feeling better, but it would be as well for her not to travel alone just at the moment. The friend she came with had to go back. Marcelle will probably drive her home in two or three days."

It was almost like a hallucination. They spoke as though nothing had happened, said the same words although there was no real bond between them.

Betty still couldn't understand why he had come. She had some difficulty in believing that he had only come to see how she was. He could have sent Florent, or even Antoine. He could even have made inquiries at the hotel desk. But he had done that anyhow. So? Why come upstairs?

Putting his hat on the carpet, he stood up. He had never been able to sit down for too long at a time, especially if he was having an important conversation with somebody, and he had to force himself not to pace up and down the room as he used to do in his office.

"I wanted to tell you something about the paper you signed. I have no intention of using it immediately."

I herewith declare that I was caught in the act by my husband and my mother-in-law, the widowed Madame Etamble, at our home at 22 bis, Avenue de Wagram, on. . . .

Everything was there, the date, the time, even the name of her accomplice which she had hesitated to reveal. The presence of her two children in the apartment was mentioned, as well as the fact that she was completely naked.

She accepted a divorce, acknowledged that Guy was the injured party, and gave up all her maternal rights.

"I've given the matter a great deal of thought. I must admit that I was concerned when I didn't hear from you for several days."

"Florent told me that."

"It was mainly to be sure that nothing had happened to you that I asked him to phone you this morning and arrange a meeting with you. It appears that you didn't want to see him."

"I was going to wait until I recovered."

"Did you have a nervous breakdown?"

"I don't know. Anyhow, it's nothing serious."

He kept his hands behind his back as he walked up and down, just as he had done when he had dictated the statement to her.

"You see, I think that, in a situation like ours, one mustn't rush things. Nobody can vouch for the future and we're not the only people involved. Mother and I talked about the whole thing at length."

Betty wrinkled her brow, her pupils contracted. She was listening, increasingly attentively.

"I don't know what you will think about it. It isn't necessarily the right solution. I suppose you realize that it would be rather awkward if you came home immediately."

She could hardly believe her ears.

"On the other hand, you shouldn't be on your own. I take it you are on your own?"

"Didn't the reception clerk tell you?"

"Yes. Besides, I thought as much. My mother and I wondered whether we couldn't make an experiment.

You would go with her to Lyons. There is no reason why she shouldn't stay in Paris until you're better. A day or two more or less doesn't make much difference. You'll spend a certain length of time with her there and then, if . . ."

He didn't finish his sentence. He was clearly embarrassed, but full of good will.

"Did *you* think of this solution?"

For Betty it was both sweet and revolting. Guy, this tall fellow pacing up and down the room, made her realize that she could return home and live with her children again. It was as though he had started to forgive her, as though he promised to forget about everything.

And it was her mother-in-law who had worked it out, who had suggested this trial period somewhat like a novitiate in a convent.

She would take her in, under her thumb. In the apartment on Quai de Tilsitt, full of memories of the general, she would watch her day in day out, recording her progress, and obviously counting on her own influence.

Betty didn't laugh, didn't show signs of indignation. Indeed, she almost shed tears.

"Did you hope that I'd say yes?"

"I don't know."

"Do you want me to?"

"I was thinking about the children, about you."

He pitied her. He had held out a helping hand in order to redeem her.

"Thank you, Guy. It's a very touching suggestion. Tell your mother, too, that I was touched by it."

"Is the answer no?"

"I think that would be better. Not so much for me as for all of you. I warned you, remember? You didn't want to listen to me."

With a single sentence she had reversed the positions. It was she who had become magnanimous, who was sacrificing herself, and, as she spoke, she glanced at the clock and wondered what was happening at Mario's restaurant.

She was afraid that her husband would stay too long and wreck everything by being there.

"You were right to come. It's just as well that we're leaving one another on a different note."

If Schwartz had been there, he would have said sarcastically:

"You're romanticizing again!"

She hadn't expected this chance, this part she had been given to play, this choice that she had been offered.

"I'll call Florent in a few days' time. You'd better leave now. Don't forget to thank your mother. It's not my fault if I hurt you, believe me. But I'm sorry, all the same."

She was taken in by it, too, and besides, she was partially sincere. It wasn't a cynical comedy. She didn't feel any attachment to Guy but, if life had been different, they might have been happy together. He could have been happy, anyhow. He could have been happy with any woman excepting her.

She didn't feel any remorse, but she felt sorry for him, nevertheless.

"You'd better leave now."

"Are you sure?"

"Yes. You'd better leave."

She was panic-stricken by the idea that Mario might arrive. Guy didn't realize that he represented a finished world from which she had broken away. She was already living somewhere else. She was sure that another life was about to begin, had already begun, or had almost begun, but it was still fragile, ill-defined.

He picked up his hat, murmuring:

"You don't need anything?"

"Nothing."

"Good luck, Betty."

"Thanks. The same to you."

He didn't know whether to give her his hand. She didn't dare hold out hers. As he went slowly toward the door, she said once again:

"Thanks."

He didn't turn around. She heard his steps fade away along the corridor and she put her hand to her forehead. It was damp with sweat.

She drank what remained of her coffee although it was cold and although there was no longer any danger of her going to sleep. Guy's visit had awakened her—that, together with the idea of The Hole, which she couldn't stop thinking about, and where she already imagined herself to be.

She was tempted to get out of bed, to go into Laure's room, look for the bottle they had opened and have a swig at it in order to get into the appropriate mood. But she mustn't smell of whisky. She must remain exactly as she had been that afternoon when Mario had tiptoed up to her bed.

She rang the bell. Even the coffeepot and the cup on the table were superfluous.

"Take them away, Jules."

"Are you going to sleep?"

"I think so."

She tried to calm herself, but didn't succeed. She was quivering with impatience and she could hardly remain in bed.

Ten o'clock . . . half-past ten. . . . They were having dinner between the red walls with English prints on them. At the bar, Jeanine's large breasts were wobbling as she laughed and passed her hands over her hips to pull down her garter belt. . . . The Negro's face was appearing in one doorway after another like a good genie. . . . Laure had finished her supper and was sipping at her glass as she watched the faces all around her and picked up snatches of conversation. . . .

Was the doctor creeping off shamefacedly to the lavatory to give himself another injection . . . Did John have a new girlfriend who was waiting for the moment to lie down on his bed while he looked at her out of his globulous eyes, sitting with a glass in his hand in his armchair where he would finally drop off to sleep . . .

She was afraid of missing her chance, of losing her

place. Mario was strong, almost brutal, yet somewhat naive. He had been intrigued by her ever since he first set eyes on her.

He had accompanied Maria Urruti to Buenaventura to protect her from her family and she had been whisked away from him under his nose. Every day he came to a quiet room in the Carlton Hotel to chat with the widow of a professor from Lyons and to give her, before he left, the pleasure that she needed just as Bernard needed his drugs.

He had known other women, all sorts of women, probably, but he had never known a woman like Betty.

Betty knew that she was all women in one. And he had suspected it. He had received her silent message and had answered it.

Why hadn't he come yet? Was Laure keeping him? Did she suspect that they had made an appointment with each other, almost in her presence?

On other evenings he went from table to table and he occasionally got into his car to drive a patron home, a crazy in a bad state, like the doctor.

He'd think of an excuse. He didn't need one. He didn't belong to Laure.

He couldn't have suspected that it was for him that Betty had just refused to go back to Avenue de Wagram. By way of Lyons, of course, as if she were on probation.

And she had told Guy to thank her mother-in-law!

Of course, it wasn't out of kindness. Betty could even reconstruct her mother-in-law's process of thought. Now she was out of that circle she was no longer inclined to be moved, only to be disgusted.

Not even that! No! There was no question of disgust at The Hole. She was past that stage. There was no possibility of return, either.

It was the end of the line.

The end of the line for the crazies! The last stop before the asylum or the morgue!

She had been wrong when she thought that the hour of the asylum or the morgue had come for her. She hadn't known that there was still The Hole, that there was still Mario. She wanted to live. She was eager to live.

She looked at the time anxiously, for she realized that it would be that night or never. She didn't want to miss her chance. She even remembered a prayer:

"O God! Make him come."

And, her body aching with impatience:

"Make him come quickly!"

She didn't add:

"And let me succeed."

She was sure she would succeed if he came, for she was so eager, so avid. But it was agonizing to be in doubt and not to have the right to budge.

She suddenly thought it would be better if she didn't have to get up and open the door. He must come in on his own, thinking he was giving her a surprise, a gift, and find her lying in the semi-darkness.

Barefoot, she hurriedly released the door giving onto the corridor, hoping that the night porter or the maid wouldn't shut it again as they went by.

Instead of the bedside lamp that gave off too much light, she lit the pale and distant light on her dressing table.

Half-past eleven . . . She wrung her hands in anxiety.

"My God! Please make him . . . "

She was tempted to make a promise in exchange. But she didn't know what to offer and she feared that it might turn against her.

She just wanted that one chance, the last one. Was it too much to ask as the price of all her efforts?

She had closed her eyes. Her thoughts were making a din in her head and she suddenly cried aloud, with a voice which came out of the depths of her throat:

"Mario!"

He was there, between the door and the bed, walking on tiptoe as he had done before, and he mischievously put a finger to his lips.

He had understood the message. He had come. He sat on the edge of the bed and, holding her by the shoulders, at arm's length, looked at her for a long time before he bent forward and pressed his cheek against hers.

"You've come!" she said, laughing and crying at the same time.

And, rubbing his cheek against hers as one animal rubs against another, he said:

"At last!"

BETTY

8

The handle of the door to the adjoining room was moving. Somebody was trying to come in. Betty hoped that Mario didn't hear: she still wasn't sure enough.

Laure, who was next door, didn't insist and the bell soon rang at the end of the corridor. She called a waiter, or the maid. There were steps, a murmur.

"Frightened?" asked Mario, his eyes close to hers.

She hesitated, knowing that she was staking all she had, and answered, trying to smile:

"No."

He squeezed her against him still more tightly and they both stopped listening. It was only much later that he murmured:

"I've got to pass by The Hole."

"I'll go with you."

"You can't. The doctor said . . ."

"The doctor doesn't know what a woman is."

She rushed over to the bureau, to the closet.

"Shall I wear a dress instead of my suit, for a change? You haven't seen me in a dress yet."

She'd need a drink when they arrived because her head was spinning.

But she didn't dress any the less quickly and dragged him out. They ran past the elevator and went down the stairs hand in hand, as if they were descending the steps of the town hall or the church.

"I've never felt so good in my life. How about you?"

"I'm happy."

It wasn't quite true yet. He couldn't help thinking of room 55 upstairs and of the forty-eight-year-old woman sitting there alone.

"Where do you live?" asked Betty.

"Above the bar. It's an old farmhouse. The second floor has a mansard roof."

The night porter watched them go by in amazement.

She was alive! She had come through! She had found a way out!

She was already taking over the car, breathing in its smell.

"I don't want any whisky tonight, just champagne. Don't worry. I won't drink too much."

The car moved off. The porter and the doorman exchanged glances. The bell rang at the porter's desk.

"Yes, Madame Lavancher . . . They've just left, yes . . . They didn't say anything to me . . . What do you say? . . . What? . . . Now . . . But it isn't possible . . . Of course, if you insist . . . We'll be up at once, Madame Lavancher. . . ."

Hanging his head, he went over to the doorman.

"You've got to come up with me and get the luggage from room 55."

"Is she leaving?"

"It looks like it. I think I know what's happened. It's that little bitch she brought along the other night who . . ."

What was the point of explaining? The doorman had seen what had happened just as well as he had.

"You'd better drive her car up."

The receptionist emerged sleepily from a little office where he lay down in the slack hours.

"What's going on?"

"A departure. Room 55."

"Madame Lavancher?"

"Yes."

"Shall I prepare her bill?"

"She didn't mention it."

In slight embarrassment, the receptionist watched

the two men go into the elevator, then automatically began to look for the file of room 55.

The doorman and the porter had to make two journeys and one could hear the car trunk opening and closing, and then the cab doors.

"Have you got a rope?"

"There's one in the boss's station wagon."

Tough luck for the boss. They'd have to have that one out with him the next morning.

Some cases were tied to the roof. Laure came down the stairs, walking stiffly.

"Tell Monsieur Raymond to send my bill to Lyons."

That was the manager.

"Very well, Madame Lavancher. I hope you'll come back soon?"

She looked at him without answering and squeezed his hand.

"Good-by, François."

She knew them all and called them all by their first names. The long lobby was empty, lit only by a few lamps, and, at the far end, behind a glass door, the dining room was in darkness.

"Good-by, Charles. Good-by, Joseph."

They didn't know what to say to her. She got into the car, lit a cigarette, and switched the engine on while the doorman still hesitated before closing the door.

"Will you be taking Route 7?"

He thought that she smiled at him in the dark. The door slammed. The gravel creaked under the tires and the car went past the gate and disappeared into the night.

•

It was only a week later, when she was looking through *Le Progrès de Lyon,* that General Etamble's widow saw that one of her neighbors had just been found dead in her apartment. With no particular emotion she said to the friend who was having tea with her:

"Did you know that Madame Lavancher has died?"

"The widow of the professor?"

"She was found dead in her bed this morning by her maid."

"I though she had left Lyons long ago. Wasn't she living in Paris?"

"In Versailles, but she had kept her apartment here and came from time to time."

"What was the matter with her?"

"The paper doesn't say."

"She wasn't very old, was she?"

"Forty-nine."

Madame Etamble suddenly remembered something. It was to Versailles that Guy had gone to see his wife. If she had been in her right mind she would surely have accepted his offer.

But it was just as well that she hadn't, just as well for everybody, especially for Guy who was still young, for Antoine and for his wife who would never really have felt at ease in the drawing room on the third floor, at night.

"I used to see her from time to time in the old days. She was a big woman, always slightly pale, but I never thought she was ill."

How could Madame Etamble have guessed that Laure Lavencher had died instead of Betty?

It was either one or the other.

Betty had won.